Also by Suzanne Kamata:

novel

Losing Kei

anthologies

Call Me Okaasan: Adventures in Multicultural
Mothering

Love You to Pieces: Creative Writers on Raising
a Child with Special Needs

The Broken Bridge: Fiction from Expatriates
in Literary Japan

The Beautiful One Has Come

Stories by Suzanne Kamata

Wyatt-MacKenzie Publishing
DEADWOOD, OREGON

for my parents

Acknowledgments

I would like to thank the editors of the following publications, where these stories originally appeared in somewhat different form:

"Havana" in *Timber Creek Review*; "Hawaiian Hips" in *Kyoto Journal*; "The Beautiful One Has Come" in Cicada, *Meridians: feminism, race, transnationalism* and *The Bookpress*; "Woman, Blossoming" in *Wingspan* and *Cicada*; "The Rain in Katoomba" in *Cicada*; "Driving" in *Wingspan* and *Crab Orchard Review*; "Mandala" in *Poesie Yaponesia* and *Wingspan*; "You're So Lucky" in *New York Stories* and *CALYX*; "The Naming" in *Ars Medica*; "Polishing the Halo" in *Wingspan*; "Bonding for Beginners" in *Tales from a Small Planet*; and "Between" in *Wingspan* and *Literary Mama*.

I'm especially grateful to Deborah Vetter and Matthew Zuckerman, who have been enthusiastic supporters of my fiction. I'm also indebted to the many friends, fellow writers, and editors who took the time to read and comment these stories in their early stages including Helene Dunbar, Japan Women Writers, Louise Nakanishi-Lind, Jo Parfitt, Andy Couturier, Ntozake Shange, and Caron Knauer. Thanks to my husband Yukiyoshi, and our kids Jio and Lilia, for giving me the time to write, and for reminding me of what is truly important. And a big domo arigato gozaimasu to my publisher Nancy Cleary for taking this project on and designing another beautiful book.

The Beautiful One Has Come:
Stories
by Suzanne Kamata

F I R S T   E D I T I O N

ISBN: 978-1-936214-38-9
Library of Congress Control Number: 2011925473

Wyatt-MacKenzie Publishing
D E A D W O O D ,   O R E G O N

www.WyattMacKenzie.com
(541) 964-3314

Requests for permission or further information should be addressed to:
Wyatt-MacKenzie Publishing, 15115 Highway 36,
Deadwood, Oregon 97430

The Beautiful One Has Come

Stories

Havana

Havana

On Hemingway's walls there are heads of animals—deer, elk, impala, and other horned beasts that Alicia cannot identify. There are books throughout the house. On the shelves next to the toilet: *Houdini* and volumes concerning the Spanish Civil War. No one has read them in decades. Those women make sure of that—the stern-faced women who sit in corner chairs, their eyes trained on Alicia as she lifts a camera to her face.

"Tsk, tsk, tsk." Behind her, Javier wags his finger. "No photo," he says.

But Alicia ignores him, puts her hand over the flashbulb, and clicks the shutter. The women rise in unison, chattering angrily in Spanish, and make X'es with their arms. For a moment, Alicia thinks that they will confiscate her camera and film and that this would make a good story when she gets back home. Then, Alicia lowers the camera, stuffs it into her tote bag emblazoned with the face of Che Guevara, and the ladies return to their chairs.

"Grumpy, aren't they?" Alicia murmurs over her shoulder. She flashes him a naughty smile, but he isn't amused. Oh, well.

She wanders to the back of the house, takes in the luxuriance of Hemingway's back yard. Is this what he looked at when he was blocked in his writing? The hills of fern and palm trees? The blooming hibiscus? For a moment the tropical splendor leaves her breathless. She takes a photo of the landscape, then moves on to the pool.

Javier has returned to the car to wait for her. She wishes that he was beside her, but his duty is as driver, not escort. He works for Nagisa, Alicia's college roommate, and her husband Jiro who works as a guard at the Japanese Embassy. Alicia is their guest.

Almost seven years have passed since Alicia stepped into that dorm room at the University of Michigan to find a slender Japanese girl unpacking her bags. She was alone; her parents had sent her on the plane by herself and Alicia had felt sorry for her. She'd looked after Nagisa during those first few months, training her to be a real American college student. Nagisa had smoked her first joint under Alicia's guidance. She'd gone to her first keg party and put on make-up for the first time. Boys had always come clamoring after the young Japanese woman who'd attended an all-girls' high school in her native country. She didn't know how to fend them off or express her interest in the ones she liked. Alicia had helped her with that, too.

Now, Nagisa is married, with two children, three-year-old Ayana, and four-year-old Tetsuya. From the letters they've exchanged over the past few years, Alicia knows that there is no great passion between Nagisa and Jiro, a paunchy man with slicked back hair, that she had chosen him because he had a good salary and a mild disposition, and because her parents approved of him. When he was transferred to this foreign outpost, she'd followed, of course. And when Nagisa invited Alicia to visit, she'd immediately booked a flight.

As an American, with the trade embargo and all, she'd had to do things on the sly. She'd flown from Michigan to Toronto to Havana. And now, here she is in the fifth day of her seven day trip, enjoying the sights.

She admires Papa's Hollywood-sized pool in solitude and snaps a few pictures of his well-preserved fishing boat and the headstones of his four cats—Black, Negrita, Linda, and Neron—and goes back to the parking area.

Alicia has never been a big Hemingway fan—all those macho stories about hunting and bullfighting and war! She has never even read *The Old Man and the Sea*, but his house was one of the few places on the tourist map that she could think of.

"Javier is yours for the day," Nagisa had told her. "He'll take you wherever you want to go."

Partly because she wanted to see more of Cuba and partly because she felt that Nagisa wanted her out of the house for awhile, she had taken advantage of the offer. Plus, she had to admit that Javier, though a bit thin, was cute. Those melted chocolate eyes! That five-o'clock-shadow-at-nine-a.m. beard!

Coming through the clearing, she sees Javier. He is sitting on a stone wall with a group of cigar-smoking taxi drivers, his shoulders comfortably slouched. When he spots her, his back stiffens like a soldier's at attention, and he moves quickly toward the car. He opens the passenger door for her and gets in behind the wheel.

After starting the engine, he turns to her expectantly. *Where to next?*

Alicia is out of ideas. They've already been to the Museum of the Revolution where Alicia saw Che's stuffed mule and the clothing of various guerillas. She's shopped the outdoor market in front of the church and loaded up on trinkets made of coconut shells. Her stomach grumbles and Alicia says "Lunch?"

There is a restaurant nearby—La Terraza—where Hemingway used to dine. Javier pulls up in front of the pale yellow building with its columns and striped awning and hurries to open the door for her. "What time?" he asks, once she is out of the car. He points to his watch and Alicia understands that he is asking when he should be back to pick her up.

She can think of nothing worse than eating alone. "No, no, no!" she says. "Please have lunch with me." She points to his chest and then to the interior of the restaurant, and then to the purse slung over her shoulder. "I'll treat you." Alicia knows that Javier can not afford lunch in a place like this on his salary. Nagisa told her that they pay him one hundred dollars a month—a generous salary by Cuban standards. He is paid in American currency, not pesos, which is a boon since most establishments accept only dollars.

Now, Javier regards her doubtfully. He shakes his head and points to the car, mimes steering. Maybe Nagisa and her husband Jiro warned him not to take advantage of their American visitor. Maybe they told him already that she wasn't used to servants and wouldn't know how to treat him.

"Please," Alicia says. "*Por favor.*" She reaches for his arm and tugs lightly and although he doesn't smile, he follows her into the restaurant.

An elderly man in a Charlotte Hornet's cap and light blue coveralls greets them at the entrance. He seems very friendly, though Alicia can't make out a word he's saying. She shakes his hand and smiles and lets him usher them to a table overlooking the sea.

"What did he say?" Alicia asks, gesturing to the white-haired man.

"Fishing." Javier mimes casting a line. "With Hemingway."

"Cool," Alicia says. Being an American, she has a healthy appreciation of celebrities and near celebrities. Once, in a restaurant, she'd sat at a table next to Picasso's grandson and she'd flown on the same plane as the singer Bobby Brown from Los Angeles to Tokyo. Here, in Cuba, she thinks it would be a thrill to meet Fidel.

The menu at La Terraza is full of fish—or fisk, as it is misprinted. Fisk in sour sauce. Fisk soup. The waitress, a curvaceous Latina with a band of sun-browned belly showing, sashays over with a pad in hand.

"I'll have this," Alicia says, pointing to something she's deduced to be shrimp on rice.

The waitress looks at Javier and he murmurs something in Spanish.

"So," Alicia says, leaning toward him on the table, menus no longer an obstruction. "Did you ever read Hemingway's novels?" She holds her hands like a book and pretends to read.

"*Si,*" Javier replies. "*El Viejo Y El Mar.*" He points to the sea.

"Ah. The Old Man and the Sea. Did you like it?"

"*Si.* I like."

A reading man. Alicia likes this about him. She suspects he's much more than the grimy handyman that Nagisa has made him out to be. She pictures him writing poetry, like Che in the mountains. Or settled at a desk, studying for an ill-paying profession.

"Do you like your job?" she asks now, feeling vaguely disloyal to her hosts.

"No," Javier says. "I don't like. But I need the money."

Aha.

"I study computers. But no money."

"Do you like Nagisa and Jiro?" Alicia asks. She primes herself for a juicy expose—reports of la señora's shopping extravagances and the master's cruelty, but Javier shrugs.

"*Sí.*"

Suddenly, as if he suspects her of ill will, a kind of veil falls over his eyes. When the food comes, he doesn't even look at her, makes no move to converse.

Alicia is convinced that at least for a moment, she enjoyed a kind of intimacy with him. She wonders what she can do to get it back.

Later, when they've run out of tourist attractions and Javier's shift is coming to a close, he drops Alicia off in front of the house. When he opens the door for her, she tucks a rolled-up hundred dollar bill into his shirt pocket.

"No, no, no," he says, plucking it out. He hands it back to her, but she refuses to take it.

"*Por favor.* It's just a teeny tiny little present. You took me all over the place today. I want to show my appreciation." She can tell he doesn't understand her quick spurt of words, but she continues, leaning closer, lowering her voice to a whisper. "Besides," she hisses. "They don't pay you enough. They're taking advantage of you." When she pulls back, there is some-thing akin to comprehension in his eyes. At any rate, when she takes the money and puts it in his shirt pocket again, he leaves it there. She steps toward the porch, tossing a little wave over her shoulder.

The kids are home from nursery school now and they greet her in the corridor.

"Come to the Barbie House," Ayana pleads, tugging on her leg.

"Let's play hide-and-go-seek," Tatsuya insists.

Alicia glances back to smile at Javier, but he is not looking at her. Instead, he is closing the gate behind him, the car already parked in the garage. Nagisa has said that he lives near by in a run-down apartment building and that he walks to work every morning in the dark.

The children, sensing her resistance, dart off into the house. Nagisa emerges from the cool marble depths of the mansion. She is wearing a bathrobe, though it's not quite five o'clock. There's not much for her to do except take mid-afternoon baths and have manicures. "So? Did you have a good time?"

"Fabulous. Javier was a great tour guide."

Nagisa raises her finely tweezed eyebrows. "He can't speak English."

"Yes he can. A little. Enough."

Nagisa covers a yawn. "Is that so?"

He speaks English and reads books by great authors, as opposed to the thick, pulpy ladies' comics that you read. He knows all about computers. He holds doors open for ladies unlike that oafish husband of yours. Alicia stifles her impatience and follows Nagisa into the living room. The TV is turned on and tuned to NHK, the national channel of Japan. Although Cubans are not allowed satellite dishes, foreigners are entitled to such luxuries.

Nagisa sinks onto the rented sofa and seems to lose herself in a commercial for Japanese noodles.

Even when they'd been university students sharing a dorm room, Nagisa had been perpetually homesick. Her mother had sent monthly supplies of her favorite soap, shampoo and snack foods. Alicia remembers sitting on the floor of their room, crunching on rice snacks while Nagisa paged through the month-old magazines sent from home. They always had funny names like *With* or *McSister* or *Orange Pages*. Alicia wonders why her friend spends so much time outside Japan when she misses it so much.

She would like to ask, would like to lapse into one of those all-night bare-all talkfests, but marriage and children and third-world living seem to have changed her. Suddenly Alicia doubts that they were ever as close as she remembers.

On TV there is now some Japanese drama. It appears that a pair of screaming women are fighting over a sheepish-looking man. A soap opera. In earlier days, Alicia had been a devotee of *All My Children*. She can relate to this, the campiness of afternoon TV.

"What's going on here?" she asks.

"An affair. The man is torn between his wife and mistress."

Alicia thinks of Jiro and wonders if he's ever picked up one of the hookers who hangs out on the street corner in front of their house. Or if he's ever lusted after the Cuban women he passes in the street.

"Did you ever want to have an affair?" Alicia asks. They'd often discussed men and sex back in college. She doesn't feel that she's out of line now.

Nagisa, however, looks at her with something bordering on irritation. "With whom?"

"A Cuban guy, for example. Some of them look very yummy."

Nagisa wrinkles her nose. "They're dirty," she says. "And they smoke those stinky cigars."

In a soap opera, Nagisa would be having an affair with the driver. Alicia wonders if Javier has ever looked upon his patroness with desire. Nagisa has a good figure—slender with long legs. She has no breasts to speak of, but she wears her clothes well. Her black hair is always shiny and swings over her shoulders.

Is Javier attracted to me? In her mind, she picks through every moment of the day, trying to come up with a significant look or gesture. The way he had opened the car door for her, the way he had bumped his knees against hers under the restaurant table.

Nagisa is once again absorbed in the TV drama and Alicia feels a surge of boredom. There is so much to do and see in Havana. Why be stuck in imaginary Japan?

"Let's go listen to salsa," Alicia says, bouncing on the sofa. "Let's go dancing."

Nagisa laughs humorlessly. "And who would take care of the kids?"

"Jiro. We'll go without him. That way we can ogle the Latinos in their tight jeans."

Nagisa rolls her eyes. "I'll ask Javier to take you. We'll pay him overtime or something."

Alicia can't believe her luck.

The following morning Alicia gets out of bed and goes to the window. She parts the lace curtains and sees that Javier is already in the driveway, washing the car.

There is a sharp rap on the door. "Alicia? Are you awake?

We're going to the market soon."

Alicia digs through her duffel bag—sweatshirt, no, denim shorts, no. She reaches into the closet for a sundress, one that will show just the right amount of cleavage. Javier should appreciate this, she thinks. By the time she has washed her face and dabbed on lipstick, Nagisa has already packed the children into the car.

Alicia remembers that when she visited Nagisa's home in Japan, she had been most interested in the mundane aspects of native life. She remembers the toilets—some with musical or heated seats—and the supermakets stocked with dried squid, pickled octopus and bean jam buns. She grabs her camera and crawls into the back seat.

Ayana scrambles onto her lap. "*Buenos dias,*" she says. "*Hola.*"

Nagisa is up front with Javier. Dark glasses hide her eyes and her red mouth is set in a grim line. She mumbles a few words of Spanish and Javier backs the car out of the driveway.

Alicia watches him in the mirror. She tries to catch his eyes, tries to arrange herself so that he can see the shadow between her breasts, but he is staring straight ahead.

At the open air market, he trails behind Nagisa, holding Ayana's tiny hand. The Cubans see the little Japanese girl and exclaim "*Que linda!*"

This early in the morning, the market is crowded with housewives. They move past the stalls of dried beans and onions and potatoes. Mounds of okra provide the only glimpse of green. There are tomatoes, too, but none of the vegetables that Nagisa had prepared the night before. For those—the long white Japanese radishes, the eggplants, the turnips—they must fly to Miami once a month.

"Beans, beans, beans," Nagisa says now, pushing through

the crowd. She finally settles on a few tomatoes and a bagful of okra. As soon as she's paid for the vegetables, she hands them over to Javier. He trails Senora obediently. Alicia's skin prickles with irritation. She would carry her own purchases. She wouldn't treat her driver like a pack horse, like a lackey.

Javier has not so much as looked at her all morning. The day before they had lunched together, had discussed literature and politics. Alicia decides that Nagisa's presence is affecting Javier's behavior. If she can get him alone again, she is sure that they will lapse back into easy familiarity.

Next, they go to a regular supermarket to buy bottled water and coffee. A guard at the entrance checks ration cards. The interior is dark and there is none of the canned music that would greet shoppers in the States, no announcements of red light specials. A mattress is on display at the front of the store. There are cases of greying meat, almost an entire aisle of different kinds of mayonnaise, but no flour, and only a little sugar although cane is grown on the island.

No wonder Javier is so slender, Alicia thinks, considering the shortage of food. Once she is back in the States, she will send him cases of rice and soup and chocolate. She will send him books and a computer—a small token of her appreciation for his generous hospitality.

On the way home, Nagisa speaks to Javier in halting Spanish. Though her phrases are broken, her voice has the tone of command. Alicia hears her name and "salsa." Javier's eyes flick to the rear view mirror, rest on Alicia's face. He nods, unsmiling. Plans have been made.

Back at the house, Javier hops out of the car and opens the door for her. She sees his gaze dive into her dress for a moment, then to the pavement.

"Thank you," she says.

He nods, then looks into her eyes at last. "I will pick you up at eight."

When Javier returns, he is dressed in a clean white shirt and black trousers. His outfit falls somewhere in between on-duty-uniform and dressed-up-for-a-date. Alicia has donned a little black number that shows off her shapely legs.

Nagisa sees her off at the door. "Have fun," she says. There is a hint of wistfulness in her voice.

Alicia squeezes her arm, feeling suddenly very grateful. "I wish you were coming, too. Remember when we used to go dancing together? That old warehouse converted into a disco?"

Nagisa nods and smiles. "I remember. Now, don't get into any trouble and keep your hands off my driver."

Alicia laughs. Could it be that Nagisa is indeed attracted to Javier? Alicia remembers college, how she was always writing down phone messages for her roommate. Young men—clean-cut fraternity brothers and burly jocks and goateed boys on the staff of the poetry magazine—were always calling for the enigmatic Asian woman. Although Nagisa had never seriously dated any American in particular, she had certainly had a busy social life.

Javier ushers Alicia to the car. He seems more relaxed.

"Do you like salsa?" she asks him.

"*Sí*. Of course."

"Do you like to rumba?"

He looks away from the road to her face for a moment. She is sitting sideways, facing him, in flirtation mode. Javier seems to understand this as he lets his gaze rest on her just a moment longer than politeness would allow. As he turns his head away, Alicia can see a smile tugging at the corner of his mouth.

"*Si*," he says. "I like rumba."

Alicia pays their way into the club, which is in a Cuban-owned luxury hotel. The waiters are nearly elderly with black jackets and red bow ties, but the clientele is young and eager to dance. Alicia can see this in the bobbing knees and the tapping toes. The crowd is waiting for the band to take the stage. Until then, they will drink and wait.

Alicia orders two *mojitos*, a kind of Caribbean mint julep. It is only after they arrive that she asks "Do you like this drink?" She has to lean close to be heard over the music.

Javier nods and raises his glass to her.

By the time the band appears on-stage, Alicia is pleasantly buzzed and ready to dance. She tugs on Javier's arm and nods toward the dance floor. Couples are beginning to gather around the stage, tattooing the dance floor with quick steps. It looks complicated, but Alicia has a few moves of her own.

She expects reluctance, but this time Javier is willing. He ushers her to the front of the stage, a hand on the small of her back. A delicious tremor runs through her body.

A French journalist wrote that Castro was wise to let Cubans keep the rumba. Here, watching bodies move in pleasure, watching the music fill the dancers, Alicia believes these words are true. Although the people of this island are deprived of religion, CNN and flour, they have this happy sexy music. For an hour or so, Alicia needs nothing else. She smiles and whoops as Javier twirls her around. He pulls her against his long, lean body for just a second, then spins her away from him. He dips her back until her dark hair nearly brushes the floor, draws her close enough for a kiss. Alicia can smell his cologne, his sweat, the rum on his breath. She feels weak for a moment, but then she is spinning once again.

When they go back to the table for a break, Alicia's bare

skin glistens with perspiration. She excuses herself to freshen up in the ladies' room. As usual, an attendant waits outside to distribute toilet paper. Alicia is feeling good. She looks into the mirror and sees her flushed cheeks and rumpled hair and knows that she is sexier than she has ever been. She tips the uniformed attendant a dollar on the way out, although twenty-five cents would have been enough.

"*Gracias!*" the woman says. She blows Alicia kisses. "*Gracias, gracias!*"

Javier has ordered drinks in her absence. He watches her cross the room, doesn't take his eyes off her until she sits down across from him.

Havana at two a.m.—waves crash and hiss against the sea wall, the lights of the Hotel Nacional shine like jewels, the moon glows up above. Alicia cracks the car window to inhale the salt-scented air.

Up ahead of them, there are three black Mercedes—something of an anomaly in this town of re-painted vintage American cars.

An arm pops out of one of the cars up ahead. A hand waves a neon wand.

"What's going on?" Alicia asks. "Are those Fidel's guards or something?" In her inebriated state, she has almost forgotten that Javier's English ability is limited at best. He mumbles something to himself in Spanish.

The hand disappears for a moment, and a man in army green squeezes out the window. He is holding an AK-47.

"What's happening?" Alicia is excited more than anything else, as if she were watching herself in a movie. This is the Cuba she'd imagined—dangerous and sexy.

Javier isn't listening to her. He puts his foot on the brake and pulls the car over to the curb. The Mercedes speed ahead and disappear into the night.

"Wow," Alicia breathes. "That was pretty scary. Feel my heart." She reaches across the car and peels Javier's fingers from the wheel. He doesn't resist as she presses his palm against her chest. She is sure that he can feel the rhythm there, the rumba of her heart.

He turns toward her then and there is something wild in his eyes that she can't read. He has made some sort of decision and now he pulls the straps of her dress over her shoulders and scoops her breasts into his hands. Alicia closes her eyes as he bends his head. She moans and pushes her nipples into his mouth. He begins sucking furiously, sending sparks to her groin. She wants to nourish him, to satisfy every hunger that he has. She wants to give him freedom and food and money.

Her dress is almost nothing, a mere scrap of fabric, and it takes less than a minute for his large hands to work it over her hips. Alicia hears the rip of black satin, but she doesn't care. She just wants to feel his skin, his breath. Her fingers fly to his shirt buttons, scramble for flesh. When his chest is bared, at last, she plants tiny kisses all over him, plucks his small brown nipples with her teeth, and he sucks in his breath.

"Javier," she whispers against his neck. "Javier." She unzips his pants and slides her hand down to grasp him.

And then they are crawling into the back seat, like teenagers at a drive-in, and Alicia is mounting him, taking him into her body, filling herself with Javier, Javier, Javier. It's like nothing she's ever experienced in her life, each rising and falling of her hips a revolution of the body. She comes with a sweet, sharp cry and feels Javier explode inside of her. The waves crash against the seawall, then recede.

For a moment, they remain in the back seat, moist skin sticking to vinyl. Alicia strokes Javier's crisp curls as she holds him against her breasts. Then he sighs and reaches for his shirt. They are silent on the drive home.

Alicia sleeps until noon. When she finally descends the winding staircase, Nagisa has coffee ready for her.

"So," she says. "How was it?"

Alicia studies her friend for a moment, wondering how much she knows. Were there stains on the car upholstery? The musk of desire clinging to the dashboard? No, Javier would have had time to clean the car out as he did every morning.

"Yes," Alicia says, accepting a cup of coffee with two hands. "Javier is a great dancer."

Nagisa raises her eyebrows. "He danced with you?"

Alicia nods, then rushes to change the subject. She senses that her old friend would disapprove of what happened by the seawall. She has decided to keep the whole thing to herself. As a diversion, she tells Nagisa about the three Mercedes and the man with gun.

Nagisa's eyes widen. "Really? That's never happened to us before. You must have been scared. I'm sorry."

Alicia shrugs. "It was exciting. I really felt like I was in Cuba."

This is the last day of Alicia's visit. She will be flying back to the States the following morning. Throughout the afternoon, she imagines her last meeting with Javier. Will they kiss? Will they exchange addresses at the airport? Could they manage a quickie in the garage?

Jiro has taken the car—and Javier—to the Embassy, so the women and children are stranded for the day. They have their nails done on the verandah by a Cuban teacher-turned-manicurist and play card games with the children. Alicia realizes that she and Nagisa have run out of things to say to one another.

Jiro is back for dinner that evening. In honor of their guest, they are having hard-to-come-by sirloin steaks and Chilean wine. Jiro fills their glasses and proposes a toast. "To our friend from far away. Have a safe journey home."

They all clink glasses and sip politely.

Then Jiro begins to tell a story about a visiting Japanese official who was staying at the Hotel Nacional, formerly a Western-owned luxury hotel. The Japanese official, it seemed, had propositioned the chambermaid.

"She told him that she couldn't have sex with him because she was working, but then he offered her one hundred dollars to let him touch her breasts." Jiro chuckles and shakes his head. "I don't know what that guy was thinking. The hotel maid!"

Alicia's heart begins beating a little faster. "So what happened?" she asks. "Did she take the money?"

Jiro nods. "Wouldn't you?"

"A hundred dollars," Nagisa mumurs. "That's a lot of money for a Cuban. Just to let a man touch her breast."

Alicia remembers the rolled-up bill she had tucked into Javier's pocket the day they visited *la Finca Vigia*.

"I saw the weather report," Jiro continues. "It looks like you'll have a good day for flying."

Alicia attempts a smile.

"We'll all go with you to the airport tomorrow," Jiro says. "We'll give you a big send-off."

"That's really not necessary. Five a.m. is so early."

"No, no. It'll be our pleasure."

In spite of the two bottles of wine that they consume at dinner, Alicia is awake half the night thinking about Javier. Did she misinterpret everything that happened between them? Was it genuine attraction on his part, or business, like that maid and businessman? Had he felt indebted to her? Was that why he had let her seduce him? Or had he even expected another tip for the sex? There is no one she dares ask.

The sky is still dark when she drags herself out of bed. Jiro helps her carry her suitcase down the stairs and loads it into the car. Although it is early, the children are wide awake, tickling each other and giggling. Nagisa has made coffee and offers Alicia a cup before departure.

Alicia peers out into the dark. The driveway is empty. "Where's Javier?" she asks. She can't help herself.

"Jiro will drive you to the airport," Nagisa says. "We decided to let Javier sleep in. He's been working overtime lately."

Working overtime? With me? Alicia is still trying to decipher the meaning of these words when Jiro starts herding them into the car. "Time to go, time to go." He is unbelievably chipper even at this hour. Alicia sits in the back seat with Nagisa and the children. She attempts to examine the upholstery, but it is dark and the children keep moving around, obscuring her view.

At the airport, Nagisa and Alicia embrace. Jiro shakes her hand.

"Come to our house again sometime," Ayana says before she disappears beyond the immigration check point. And they all laugh because they know that she won't be back.

Hawaiian Hips

Hawaiian Hips

*B*efore Victor arrives, we are bored. Three years have passed since the Great Hanshin Earthquake; a year and a half since royalty's last visit. And there hasn't been a political scandal of eyebrow-raising proportion in quite a while. The last town councilman to get into trouble was a sixty-five-year-old bookseller—a man with a blue-haired wife, children educated in Tokyo, and five grandchildren. This man had been having an affair with a seventeen-year-old girl. The girl, whose name was never disclosed because of her age, had another lover at the same time—a company president in the neighboring city. When our local councilman found out about the other guy, he went crazy. He threatened to kill his rival. He stalked him for weeks and made menacing phone calls. And that's what he was arrested for—the threats. I thought at the time that he'd never recover his status in the community. Our town is small; there is nowhere to hide. The man's bookstore was shut down. He resigned from public office. And though he was seen walking his feather-tailed dog, he laid low for a year. His constituents forgave him (he'd helped them repair their roofs after the last big typhoon) and the incident with the girl was forgotten. The man was later re-elected. Nothing much has happened recently.

Five years ago, I was the big event in this island town at the edge of the Inland Sea. When I stepped off the ferry with my new husband, Toshiki, tongue-wagging reached an all time high. "Look at that yellow hair!" they said. And, "What a big nose she has!" Most of the children had never seen a flesh-and-blood foreigner before, though they were familiar with Mariah Carey and Michael Jordan. And the adults, well, some of them had encountered soldiers during the war, but I was the first American to move into the neighborhood with long-term plans.

In those days, little old ladies took an anthropological interest in the contents of my grocery basket. "*Sakana,*" they'd mumble, peering at the slabs of pink tuna under plastic warp. "Are you going to eat that raw?" Or, "Steak," they'd say, spotting a hunk of beef. "Just as I'd expected." I caught children swiping T-shirts from my clothesline and picking through my trash. People spoke to me in baby words though I'd spent six years studying Japanese and worked as a translator.

I did my best to blend in. When the neighbors gathered to pull weeds and pick up garbage at six o'clock on the first Saturday morning of the month, I was there with them. I enrolled in *ikebana* classes and *tai chi.* Gradually, the townspeople got used to me. They no longer check to see what brand of toilet paper I buy.

In early June, as I am leaving the *ikebana* class at the town hall, I'm halted by a bright sign on the bulletin board. "Hula Lessons!" it says in fat red letters inked on yellow construction paper. "Authentic Hawaiian Teacher!" Beneath, in proper black calligraphy, more detailed information appears in Japanese. Hula—this is something new. Of course I sign up.

The first class is on a Tuesday night in one of the tatami rooms at the town hall. The other twelve ladies—mostly housewives in their fifties and one younger woman named Akiko- and I leave our shoes at the door and slide our stockinged feet onto the sweet-smelling reed mats. There is no one else here, no teacher, no note, no indication that anything will happen at all.

We are sitting there moaning about the endless rain and the coming heat of summer. We are talking about the weather and wondering what we will cook for supper. And then a figure appears in the doorway—a young Polynesian with black hair rippling over his shoulders. He is wearing a shirt printed with huge, red flowers. Our Hawaiian has arrived.

"Good evening lovely ladies." He slips out of his sandals and steps onto the mat.

His eyes hone in on me. He smiles and his teeth are dazzling against tanned skin. "A fellow American," he says. "Fabulous."

The ladies start clucking. I can hear them trying to translate our brief exchange. "They already know each other?" one woman asks another. "They were friends in the U.S.A.?"

I will explain to the ladies later. Now, I address the young man. "You can't wear shoes on the mats," I say. "You'd better take them off and leave them at the door."

He struts to the center of the room. "I am Victor," he says, pointing to his chest. Then he bends at the waist, and we bow, too.

"I thought all Hawaiian men were big," one woman tells me at the end of that first class. "Big like Akebono." In Japan, everyone knows about the refrigerator-sized sumo wrestlers bred in the islands. Compared to them, Victor is delicate. Petite. His shoulders are no wider than mine. His jeans would cut off my circulation.

Victor is too small for me. I never dated men who weighed less than I did. I married a man who could carry me over the threshold, who could haul sandbags in a storm. But I agree with the others that Victor is beautiful.

The next time I see him, he is frozen in front of the vegetables at the local supermarket. He stands there, hands on hips, head cocked, as if awed by all those green leaves.

"Victor," I say.

He turns at the sound of my voice. "Beth! Oh, thank the Buddha!" he says, thumping his heart. "You can save me!"

"From what?" I ask uneasily. The carrots, the freshly spritzed spinach, the shrink-wrapped shiitake—it all looks so harmless.

"It's my lover's birthday and I promised to him make dinner," Victor says, "but I have no idea what to do with these things." He picks up a package of bamboo shoots, then puts it back. He dangles a long, slender root.

Victor is gay? I freeze my facial muscles so as not to show my surprise. "That's burdock," I say. "You can stir fry it or shred it for a salad."

He seems just as perplexed as before. I get the idea that he doesn't know how to cook.

"Why don't you take him out to dinner?" I say. Then I

name a couple of good restaurants.

"That's just it." Victor frowns. "He isn't ready to be seen in public with me. He's worried about what people will think."

I'm worried too, though I don't say as much. Around here, while men in make-up and "new-half" transsexuals are often seen on TV, they don't exist in real life. Maybe Victor should keep his relationship a secret.

I sense that Victor is lonely and about to tell me his life story. Although no one can understand us, it seems a bit risky to discuss his lover in the midst of shopping housewives. We should be having this conversation in the corner booth of a coffee shop. I'm about to suggest that we go someplace private when one of the ladies from the hula class comes from around the corner. "Vik-tah!" she shrieks. Victor nods in return.

The woman assesses the situation—a single man without a woman to take care of him—and leads him to the prepared food. There, he loads his basket with pumpkin salad, grilled fish, and pickled seaweed. Then, she ushers him into line at the cashier.

I realize that he will not be able to disentangle himself, so I slip away. "See you on Tuesday," I call out. Both Victor and the woman wave.

When we arrive at seven-thirty, ten minutes before our teacher, the older women urge Akiko toward the front.

"He doesn't want to look at us old ladies," the older women say. "Let him enjoy you, like a flower."

Akiko blushes. She demurs. She heads for the back.

"No, no, no," the ladies say. They push her the other way.

At twenty-five, Akiko is the youngest woman in our hula class. Her face is scrubbed clean and her hair sprouts from her head in wiry pigtails, like Pippi Longstocking. She wears dresses that crawl up her neck and cover her knees. I'm willing to bet money that she is a virgin. The rest of us are long-married, and the only romance we're bound to find is on TV or in novels. If we're lucky, we might get a vicarious thrill via Akiko.

Victor is always late. We practice while we are waiting. Each of us, in our own bubble, dreams of ukulele music, palm trees in the wind. We make fog with our arms. We plant flowers with our hands. We move our hips from side to side and toss nets into the sea.

"Good evening, lovely ladies." Victor comes into the room. He doesn't speak Japanese, but this doesn't seem to matter. This is dance, after all. Words are not so important. In a bind, Victor will ask me to translate. When he does, I see the ladies' eyes darken. They do not want to listen to me. They'd rather look at Victor with his burnished skin and Kona coffee eyes.

"Sorry I'm late," he says. He has brought a tape player and his ukulele. He has taken off his shoes and rolled up his white trousers. We can see the tip of a tattoo on his calf. We wonder what it is.

First, Victor tells us to warm up. He puts on a tape—a slow song, something that I used to make out to in college. He rolls his head around in a circle, slowly, and we watch the ripple of his hair.

It's summer. The room is hot. Victor untucks his shirt. Unbuttons it. Ties it around his waist. We can see his washboard stomach. He wears a shark's tooth necklace under his shirt.

"Let's do "Koke'e," Victor says. This is the song we've been dancing to for three weeks now. It's a song about a beautiful place. As we dance, we try to imagine volcanoes, hibiscus, the cerulean sea.

Victor dances with us, then tells us to dance by ourselves. He plays the ukulele. He watches us.

"Akiko, you move your hips very well," he says. He looks straight at her. Her gaze falls to the floor.

I know that she is smiling. She is hoping, maybe. The other women smile, too. Their little ploy is working, they think. They do not know that Victor is gay. They are probably starting to believe that he will stay in this town and teach us hula forever.

At the end of the class, Victor approaches me. "Wanna go for a beer?"

Out of the corner of my eye, I can see Akiko's head droop. The ladies exchange glances with each other. They frown behind my back.

"Umm, okay," I say. "I'll meet you out front."

Everyone knows that I am married. My husband is Japanese. He is a good man, people say. He is very handsome. There is no reason for the wife of such a man to be dissatisfied. People worry, though, that one day I will tire of international marriage, that I will leave my husband for one of my own kind. It's not good for me to be seen with Victor, but he is the only other American in this town.

I think that Victor needs me more than I need him. I can speak Japanese. He only knows a few words. I have a husband, a job and a house. No one knows, exactly, what Victor does. Or what he has. I think he is being kept.

I wait for him outside the town hall, which is where we gather each week. The other women brush past me. They don't say "good-night." When I see Akiko, I suddenly feel guilty.

"He just wants to speak English for a little while," I say. "He isn't interested in me."

I have said too much, I know. Akiko blushes. It's dark, but I know that she is blushing.

When Victor appears at last, his shirt buttoned against mosquitoes, he drapes a hand over my shoulders. I check to make sure no one is looking.

There is a kid squatting in the telephone booth on the corner. He's got the receiver to his ear. There is a man walking his dog.

"Come on, let's go," I say. I start walking fast. I feel as if I'm about to do something illegal.

We duck into a little mom-and-pop bar across the street. We order beer. The proprietor brings us one big bottle and two small glasses. I pour for Victor, then he fills my glass.

"Is something wrong?" I ask

"My lover," he sighs. "He says it's time to get married."

I consider this. Gulp down three swallows of beer. "In Japan? Are same sex marriages legal here?"

Victor shakes his head. "No, I mean to a woman. His parents are pressuring him. They've already got a girl lined up. They want him to carry on the family line and he thinks it's the right thing to do."

"Is he the oldest son?" I ask.

"The only son."

"Ah." I'm wondering if Victor knows about Jiro's role in the family. He is probably expected to settle in this town, in his parents' hard-won house, and to tend their graves when they are gone. He is the heir, after all. There are young people around here who have sacrificed true loves and grand dreams to satisfy their parents. My own husband Toshiki had a crack at a career in professional baseball, but he gave it up to take over his father's business.

I don't know too much about Victor's lover. What I do know is this: He is Japanese. They met in Hawaii. Victor has followed him back to Japan, to this little town surrounded by onion fields.

"Then what would happen to you?" I ask. I don't know if this is the proper question. I'm not good at counseling.

"I'd be like his concubine. I'd be uncle to his children." Victor's voice is saturated with sarcasm. He drains his glass, and refills it himself.

I glance at the proprietor. I don't want him to think that I have bad manners, that I am not keeping Victor's glass filled. Self service—this is the way we do it in America, I'd like to say, but no one is really paying attention.

I think of Akiko. "What if you got married, too?"

Victor looks at me as if he can't believe what he's hearing. "Hello?" he says. "I'm gay."

I shrug. "That's what they do here. It worked for Yukio Mishima."

For a couple years, Victor tells me, he lived in San Francisco. He liked to watch the fog lift from the bay each morning, liked the roller coaster streets and the gorgeous, available men, but he started missing the islands and so he went back to Maui. His parents were happy to see him. Later, they invited him to bring his new lover home for dinner.

"I'm not ashamed of my identity," Victor tells me. "I know what I'm about. But Jiro is still in the closet. He's afraid he'd be stoned to death or something."

I can tell by the way he drinks, by the furrows on his forehead, that Victor is in pain. The agony of love is hard to conceal. I listen to his story and pour him another drink because I want to help him, but I am secretly thrilled. This is better than a soap opera.

On the following Tuesday, when I enter the classroom, the women turn their backs to me. I greet them loudly, but they merely grunt in return. Akiko has not yet arrived. I wonder if she is crying at home, mooning over Victor. Sticking pins into a voodoo doll of me.

It doesn't help when Victor arrives, an aloha shirt billowing around his torso. Everyone sees him wink at me. Then he nods to the ladies and smiles, showing his perfect teeth

I cower at the back of the room. The ladies communicate with eyes and eyebrows. They bump into me and don't apologize.

And then the door slides open and Akiko steps out of her shoes. We can see her legs for the first time and they are not half bad. She is wearing a skirt that pulls tight across her buttocks. I'm afraid that it will rip if she bends over. On top, she is wearing a knit shirt and I see that she has breasts. The neckline scoops and reveals a chest shiny with perspiration. I can smell her perfume from the back of the room. She cuts her eyes at me and takes her place front and center.

Victor teaches us how to make fish with our hands. With fingers pressed together, we layer right hand on left. Then we make our hands undulate with the waves. Victor plays his ukulele and sings about beautiful places. We make the rain fall with our fingers. We move our hips in half-circles.

At the end of the class, when the ladies are gathering up their purses and the song sheets, the cassette players they use to trap Victor's voice, he takes a few steps toward me.

Tonight, I think, I should turn him down. I live in this town, after all. I cannot afford the rumors. This cold war is freezing my heart. I decide to say "no," but before Victor can make his way to me, Akiko steps in his path.

"*Sensei*," she says, using that honorific word for teacher. "Would you like to have a cup of coffee with me? I treat you."

She says this loud enough for everyone to hear, though I am the only one besides Victor likely to understand. Suddenly, I think I know why she was late. Not only was she busy putting on make-up and pasting tight clothing to her curves, but also she was memorizing this phrase. Didn't I tell her that English was the key?

I expect Victor to turn her down gently with talk of a headache or fatigue. Instead, to my great surprise, I see him nod. He follows Akiko out the door without saying good-bye to me.

I want to run after them. "Oh, foolish girl," I will say, "He is toying with you. This Victor is going to break your heart."

I want to rescue her, but I know how it would all look to the other ladies. They would think I was trying to guard him for myself, so I sigh and gather my things as well. On the way out, I say "*sayonara*." The ladies answer back, a little warmer than before.

The next week, I wait outside for Victor. I stand there ten minutes in the sticky evening air. First I hear his whistle, then I see him coming down the sidewalk, hair flowing in the breeze, arms laden with supplies. I jump out in front of him.

"I wanna talk to you," I say.

"Beth," His step is springy. His smile is wide. "I've got great news."

"It's about Akiko," I say, not willing to be interrupted.

"Oh, Akiko. She's a great kid. I'm teaching her English."

"Are you sure?" I ask. "Does she know that?"

Victor ignores me. He is walking so fast that I can barely keep up. "I have to tell you something," he says. "Jiro and I are going to buy a houseboat together and live in Amsterdam. He's decided that he truly loves me."

I have never met him, but I believe that Jiro has simply been dreaming out loud. I fear for Victor's heart. I don't say this.

And then we are at the door of the classroom and the women are watching, so the conversation ends and I ease myself away.

On this night, Akiko is wearing a red leather mini-skirt and a see-through blouse. A black bra is visible underneath. There is a desperation in her dress

Akiko has taken the hula to new heights, I think, watching her from the back row. Or maybe new lows. She is gyrating with eyes closed. If she were wearing a grass skirt, it would be wilting from the heat. It would be crackling, no doubt, blazing around her hips.

At the end of the class, Akiko and Victor leave together. They leave as if they'd made arrangements in advance. This goes on for weeks and my curiosity grows like a tumor.

One evening, I can't stand it anymore. I dawdle in the classroom, practicing the *kaholo* (side to side step with hip movement). I wait until all the ladies have gone home by scooters and bicycles and husbands' car. When the coast is clear, I creep outside, cross the street, and sneak into the mom-and-pop bar.

The proprietor nods and directs me to the back. He's seen me with Victor, the other American, and figures we are a set.

I approach on tippy-toes and, at first, I can't tell which one is Victor. Akiko, I know well enough. I have stared at her recently bared legs and wiggly bottom from the back row for many weeks now. I'd know that black bra anywhere. But the other two, on either side of her, look like twins from behind.

Their hair is the same shoulder-sweeping length, the same light-swallowing black. They both wear aloha shirts—ginger blossoms backed by pink. And then one turns, and notices me, and I see that he is Japanese. Jiro, I think. Who else could it be?

I doubt Akiko would welcome me, and Victor would know that I am spying. I backtrack without being spotted by the others and burst into the night.

Six weeks later, I'm sitting on the sofa next to Toshiki. We're watching TV and drinking beer when the doorbell rings.

I rush to the door and fling it open, expecting some wild surprise. Lo and behold, it's Victor. We haven't spoken in over a month.

"If you're selling macadamia nuts, we don't want any."

Victor pushes past me and into the house. He forgets to take off his shoes. He is a whirling dervish, a muttering madman. I grab his shoulder and shove him into a chair.

"Okay," I say. "Tell me what's wrong."

"It's Jiro," he says. "He's changed his mind about the houseboat."

Victor talks for hours and I just nod and hum. It's obvious that Jiro can not make up his mind. Gay or straight, Japan or Hawaii, sushi or spaghetti, the news or the prison drama on channel three—Jiro can never choose.

"Maybe you should give him an ultimatum," I say. "Make him decide one way or the other so you can get on with your life."

My advice is so simple, but Victor nods through his tears. "That's it, Beth. You're absolutely right."

A few days later, we are once again gathered for hula. I'm at the back, as always, and Akiko is at the front. We have more or less mastered the *kaholo,* the *ka'o,* the *hela* and the *ami.* We know all the moves to "Koke'e."

"Fabulous," Victor says, when we become still. "You ladies are ready for a luau." Although Victor has been in Japan for three months now, he continues to address us solely in English.

This class seems like any other. We sway to Victor's ukulele and the screech of cicadas, then stretch and gather our things. Victor leaves ahead of the rest of us, Akiko trailing behind. I wait until the room has emptied and turn off the lights. I push through the door and into the hot breath of the evening.

The women are still there, gathered on the sidewalk. Akiko stands away from the rest. They are staring at the phone booth. I look too. At first all I can see is black hair and flowers—the hibiscuses on Victor's shirt—smooshed against the glass. He's making a phone call, I think. So what? But then I notice fingertips poking through the hair and Victor tries to shake them free. But wait. It's not Victor. The head turns and I catch a glimpse of Jiro's face and it's smeared with tears. Then I see that there are two heads of black hair, two pairs of legs jostling for space. There are four hands—the two in Jiro's hair and the two batting at Victor.

Jiro squirms, but Victor is stronger. He's in control here. He pulls his fingers out of Jiro's hair and with one wipes a tear from Jiro's face. Licks it. And then his mouth is moving forward, forward, crashing into Jiro's mouth. And they are kissing. Or rather Victor is kissing. Jiro is trying to get away.

It occurs to me that this is Victor's last ditch effort, and I feel a little sick to my stomach. This is worse than a hand on my shoulder or shoes in the house. Victor has gone too far this time.

I can hear Akiko crying softly and the hiss of women's whispers. I hear a siren in the distance and imagine that someone is coming to arrest Victor. Arrest him for revealing Jiro's secret. This is not a thing for watching, but I know that Victor wants us to see. Although I want to turn away, my attention is pulled taut and my shoes are stuck to the sidewalk.

Then there is a shifting of bodies in that glass box—an upper-cut punch, I think—and a squeak of the door. Victor's lover escapes. He dashes away from Victor's mouth and fingertips and disappears around a corner. I worry that he is headed for a bridge or a tall building. Or train tracks. But in the morning, the news is not grim. The sun rises, as ever before.

Without being told, I know that Victor is gone.

Of course, there are no more hula lessons. We are no longer a group. We float apart and go back to our separate lives, sometimes sharing moments in the vegetable department at the grocery store, or at the post office waiting to buy stamps. I learn that Akiko is pregnant. She has married someone named Jiro. And a bigger train station will be built next spring.

At first I think that Victor has vanished without a trace and that everything is once again as before. But then one day I find a post card in my mailbox—no message, just a photo of Hanauma Bay. And then I go for a ride on my bicycle and I hear the twang of ukulele strings coming from a field. I look across the onion plants and see a small cassette player and a woman in a bonnet, swaying her hips, and carving mountains in the air.

The Beautiful One Has Come

The Beautiful One Has Come

All night long I watch the planes crash into the twin towers. And crash again. The balls of fire, the plummeting bodies, the sudden sag of skyscrapers. All night I watch the broadcasts from America on television and think of Nefertiti.

This is what I know of that Egyptian queen: It is said that she was a princess from another land. She was the wife of Akhenaten, and the mother of six daughters. She and her husband started a new religion. But then she suddenly disappeared from public record.

Some scholars believe that she was banished, perhaps for defying Akhenaten in matters of religion. She might have died. All agree, however, that she was beautiful. Drawings and statues attest to this. And then there is her name. Nefertiti: "the beautiful one has come."

I know these things because of my sister, Reina. She loved to talk about Nefertiti. One might even say that she was obsessed. In her room, there were piles of books: *Sun Queen*, *Monarchs of Ancient Egypt*, *The Great Royal Wife*. And on and on.

Once, for a Halloween party, she copied Nefertiti's distinctive headdress and lined her eyes with kohl. She had large, double-lidded eyes, unlike my tiny narrow ones, and with her salon tan, I swear she belonged on a barge floating down the Nile.

She liked to remind people that "Reina" was close to the French word for queen, "la reine," or the Indian "ranee," but my parents had not been thinking that at all when they named her.

Mother was more concerned with the fortune-teller's advice regarding the number of strokes in each Chinese character. She was told that Misaki, the name she had originally chosen, would result in bad luck for her as-yet-unborn daughter.

My parents did not understand Reina's preoccupation with Nefertiti. They had little interest in foreigners or their countries.

"Why don't you study about Jingu?" our father asked, referring to Japan's ancient empress.

She just mocked him for his provincialism and mailed off an application to the American University in Cairo.

My parents worried that my sister would transfer her passion for Nefertiti to some dark-skinned man and stay in Egypt forever.

When her acceptance letter arrived, Reina called a family meeting. We gathered in the room just off the foyer, the one with sofas where we entertained guests. Reina sat across from our parents, her knees pressed together, her back straight. I sat next to her in a slouch.

"I've made up my mind," she said. "I'm going to Egypt."

"Why don't you apply someplace closer to home?" Father pleaded. Behind his glasses, his eyes glistened with tears. "You could probably get into Keio or Waseda with your test scores. You might even be accepted at Tokyo University."

Tokyo University—more popularly known as Todai—was the most prestigious college in all of Japan.

Mother knotted her fingers together and nodded along.

I didn't move. My tongue was paralyzed. I stared at the opposite wall where a calendar featuring the Emperor and his family was hung.

"Todai grads are a bore," Reina said, tossing her hair. "Look at all those crusty old men running the country. And the younger ones think like old fogeys."

"Well, you don't need to go all the way to the Middle East," Father insisted. "Japan is safer—the safest country in the world, I'll bet."

That night, as we lay in the dark on our side-by-side futons, away from our parents, Reina said, "This country is suffocating. I need to have some adventures."

Finally, our parents gave in.

To show her gratitude, Reina hung around the house most of that spring and summer, helping Mother with the housework and cooking, and charming Father with her stories.

Two nights before she left, she had a big party with her friends, and the following evening, we went out to eat as a family.

We went to a seafood restaurant overlooking the Yoshino River because Reina loved blue fin tuna sushi and she didn't think she'd have a chance to eat it in Cairo. We sat on cushions around a long, low table covered with dishes of exquisitely prepared food—platters of raw fish adorned with tiny flowers, egg custard with pine nuts, seaweed salad drizzled with vinegar dressing.

Reina, resplendent in a red silk dress, went around the table pouring drinks for each of us.

Mother wore black. She sighed and said, "I hope they at least have rice over there."

Those are the inane kinds of things we talked about as we tended our private thoughts. My parents were probably wondering if they'd ever see Reina again. I was just trying to store up a few extra memories of my adored older sister. When she came back, she'd be different; that, I knew for sure. Maybe I wouldn't even like her anymore.

As her plane took off, I tried to follow her in my imagination. I tried to picture the insides of the jet (blue seats?), the faces of the airline attendants (not too difficult, since she was flying on a Japanese airline), the food served at each meal (somewhat baffled, I could only come up with rice and fish).

All that day of her departure and into the next, I tried to guess her state of mind (scared, but excited) and the fresh sights. She'd see camels, I figured. Pyramids. An ocean of sand.

A week later, Reina filled in some of the details in her first letter from Egypt: "Dear Mom, Dad, and Mika, I'm finally here in the land of pharoahs and mummies and Nefertiti!"

Father read her letters out loud after dinner when we were sitting at the table drinking green tea. Her words were better than dessert, and I savored them for days afterward.

The letters were usually written to all of us, although my

parents and I wrote separate replies. Finally, six months after she'd gone, a thin blue envelope arrived, addressed only to me.

Mother handed it over with a greedy look in her eyes, but I ignored it and took the letter to my room, the room I had once shared with Reina. I turned it over in my hands a few times, letting my anticipation build. The stamp featured a distinguished-looking man with a flat-topped round cap. The letter was postmarked Cairo, a week before.

I brought the envelope to my nose and inhaled deeply, trying to detect a trace of Egypt—some exotic scent like camel dung or rose attar, but all I could smell was ink.

At last, I slit the envelope open and pulled out Reina's letter.

"Dearest Mika,

I am in love!

You must promise not to breathe a word to Mom and Dad, but I will tell you all. His name is Hassan and he's a student like me. Gorgeous, like a desert prince, a gentleman, and a poet!"

Part of me felt privileged to be taken into her confidence, to be trusted with the secrets of her heart. But another part of me went cold with dread. It was just as our parents had feared. Reina would marry this man and stay in Egypt and we would never see her again.

I thought that I should tell my parents right away. Maybe they would force her to come home before a wedding could take place. It would be for her own good, I thought. Love was making her crazy. She'd lost all reason. After all, hadn't she herself written that women stayed behind veils and walls, that they were not permitted the same freedom as men? It was worse than Japan!

But then a few months later, she stopped writing about Hassan. She never explained what had happened.

When Reina finally came back for good at the end of four years, she became an English teacher. What else could she do with a degree in Egyptian History in a backwoods prefecture like ours?

All day, she explained gerunds and infinitives to fidgeting high school students. We hoped that she would blend into this new life, but I think that her mind was flitting beyond the hydrangea bushes outside the classroom, across oceans and continents. She told us that she was happy.

She discovered the International Society, a local organization that put on monthly cooking parties. One time, they prepared Indian food. The next, the theme was the Middle East. Reina attended the session and made some Egyptian friends.

Ahmed was a student at the local university and his young wife Nabib was along for the ride. Reina started spending all of her free time with them. She even invited them to our house for dinner once. Reina did the cooking.

Father and Mother greeted them at the door. I stood behind them.

Ahmed had caramel-colored skin and curly black hair. His wife wore a floaty blue scarf over her head.

Father tried to shake Ahmed's hand, but he bowed instead, like a Japanese vistor.

When Mother offered to take Nabib's scarf, she shook her head and yanked it down tighter, as if it might blow away. She wore it even at the dinner table.

"What did you say this was?" Father asked, picking at a bean croquette with his chopsticks.

"*Tammia*," Reina said, popping a forkful into her mouth. "I loved these when I was in Cairo."

Nabib nodded. "They are just like my grandmother used to make."

Mother gamely made her way through the meal, nibbling on prunes stuffed with walnuts and cheese pastries, but Father gave up when the mint tea arrived.

"This is too sweet," he said. "Give me some green tea."

Mother quickly got up to shake some tea leaves into a pot.

Reina didn't seem offended. She just rolled her eyes at me. When Nabib and Ahmed said that it was the best meal they'd ever had, my sister beamed like a hundred suns.

In early January, Reina announced that she was in need of a live chicken. "My friends need it for Ramadan," she said. "Do you think that Uncle could spare one of his hens?"

Father's brother lived in the mountains of Tokushima. He grew tangerines and kept a small brood of pullets. We hadn't visited him in several months, but Father agreed to call him.

The following weekend, we were all packed into a car— Reina, the two Egyptians, Mother, Father, and me. I tried not to gasp as we swerved along the narrow, curvy, mountain roads. There were no guardrails, and the dense brush on the side of the mountain seemed to go on forever. If we went off the road, we would be lost in the brambles and no one would ever find us.

Suddenly, a truck whooshed into view, coming around the curve as if its brakes were gone. Father wrenched the steering wheel, taking us off the pavement for a moment, cracking sticks under the tires. When the truck passed us, the car swayed. And then it was just whipped up dust behind us and I heard a chorus of sighs.

Only Ahmed seemed unruffled. "Allah is protecting us." His voice was sure and calm.

Reina murmured in agreement.

While my heart was still banging against my ribs, I had a thought that was almost more disturbing than our near-death. What if my sister was changing religions? If she converted to Islam, would she be able to take part in our family rituals for *Obon* and the New Year? Or would her new beliefs make her a stranger to us?

I thought that it would be difficult, at best, to have to always be driving into the mountains for live chickens, to have to kneel and pray when the mullah's call sounded in your head, even if you were in the middle of Sogo department store.

I fretted about these things for the rest of the ride, right up until we stood in Uncle's yard, watching Ahmed wring the hen's neck with his bare hands.

I shouldn't have worried. A few months later, Reina brought home a man who was nothing like Ahmed. He was Japanese. He wore a navy wool suit and a tie. He was from a family that processed indigo leaves for dyers—a clan steeped in tradition—though he himself worked at a company that created computer software.

They'd met through friends, Reina explained. They were going to get married.

When they looked at each other, their eyelids became droopy with desire. I recognized that gaze from Hollywood movies, but I'd never seen it anywhere else till then. And even when they were separated by the length of a room, they seemed to be dancing together. So this is love, I thought.

I wasn't sure what drew them together. Maybe some animal call, or something beyond science. Karma. At any rate, they didn't seem to have much in common. He was not especially interested in Nefertiti, or anything else foreign, for that matter. His only trip abroad had been a group tour to Guam a year before. Even so, he promised Reina a honeymoon in Egypt.

The wedding was quite an affair. My sister in silk kimono, first the hooded white one to hide horns of jealousy (though I doubted the groom, so transparently enamored of his new wife, would ever do anything to make those horns sprout), then the blazing red one with its embroidered silver crane. We all ate and drank to ten thousand years of happiness for the newlyweds. In speeches, friends and mentors made wishes for their children, their shining future together.

Reina sat at a long cloth-draped table at the front of the room. Her black hair, piled atop her head, was set off by a gilded folding screen. Nothing had such luster as she did on that day.

After the kimono, she changed into a simple black velvet gown and tiara. And I, having joined in quite a few toasts, turned to the family friend seated at my left and said, "You know, Reina means 'queen' in French.'"

It is early morning and now there is just smoke and rubble and tears on the TV screen. I hear a door slide open and Mother shuffles into the room.

"Turn it off," she says. "Go to sleep." She runs her hand over my hair.

But when I crawl into my futon, I can't rid myself of those images. The planes. The tall buildings. The dust, and fear.

The blue sky.

It all starts to get mixed up with scenes of the temple at Luxor. The tour bus. The honeymoon couples. The men with machine guns who jumped out from behind ancient stones.

And then there was the postcard that arrived a week later: "I have never been so happy in my life."

The card, with its view of barques on the Nile, is still propped against the family shrine. A black and white portrait of Reina looks down from the wall above.

By the time I wake up the next morning, Mother has already set out a bowl of rice and a cup of green tea next to the postcard. I go into the kitchen and cook up a few bean croquettes, and then I put a plateful of those there, too.

Woman, Blossoming

Woman, Blossoming

"Thank you honorable guests for coming here on this day when you are surely very busy, to pay homage to the great Taizo Saijo who was born in this very prefecture…"

Yoshiko Saijo stands off to the side listening to the curator drone. In her pigeon-grey kimono, with her hair pulled into a tight ball, she looks the picture of propriety. The artist's widow. The dignified dowager.

"…works gathered from collections in Europe and Japan, some never publicly exhibited until this day…"

Yoshiko looks out at the gathering. She sees wrinkled men in berets, one with long white hair. Another leans on a cane. One or two seem a bit familiar. Had she known them in Paris? That was so long ago.

"And now, would you kindly do the honors?"

All eyes turn to Yoshiko. The curator holds a pair of scissors in his white-gloved hands, a red ribbon festooning the handle.

Yoshiko reaches out with both hands. She takes the scissors, bows and snips the tape. "Please take a look," she says, gesturing to the gallery where her late husband's paintings are hung

The guests flow toward the first painting, completed when Taizo was still a student. It is of a field—a Japanese field, perhaps, not unlike the one near the house where Yoshiko had grown up. The one where she had started her career.

"Yoshiko!"

Yoshiko hunched down lower, her back scraping against a tree trunk. She knew that she was supposed to be at home, washing the rice for supper and helping to keep track of her five younger brothers and sisters, but she wanted to finish this drawing. Just that rambling fence...

She got so lost in her sketch that she didn't see her mother until she was standing over her. Her shadow fell across the page and then the sketchbook was snatched out of her hands.

"Lazy girl! There are mouths to be fed and clothes to be scrubbed and here you are making pictures!"

Yoshiko held her breath, bracing herself for the rip and crumple of paper. She'd spent hours on it. This was her best one yet.

But her mother didn't tear up the drawing. Not this time. She gave it a long hard look—the sweet potato field, the plough, the houses crowded together in the distance—and grunted. Then she slammed the book shut and yanked her daughter by the elbow till she was standing.

Yoshiko followed her home.

Later that evening when the dishes were washed and the

youngest children tucked into their futons, her father called out to her.

"Yes, *Otosan?*"

He sat by the brazier, smoking and drinking sake from a small pottery cup. He held Yoshiko's notebook open on his knees.

"Did you do this?" His voice was gruff, but his eyes were kind.

"Yes, Father." Yoshiko lowered her gaze.

"Then I think we need to send you to school."

At the Tokyo Institute of Art, the halls were full of young men with Rembrandt beards and baggy clothes. They all looked as if they'd stepped out of a Dutch painting. Yoshiko didn't fit in. She wore a *hakama* and her hair hung in a neat braid down her back. She had no interest in painting dykes and tulips. She was partial to chrysanthemums.

In her first class, she was assigned a seat near the back. She could see all of the other students in their almost identical outfits. There were only a few girls, quiet and shy like herself.

The professor passed out a number of prints by the artist Vermeer— a girl reading a letter.

"You will copy this," the professor said.

Yoshiko prepared her colors.

"This is old stuff," the young man next to her muttered, "Why not Monet? Why not Degas?"

Yoshiko stole a glimpse of the student. He had a sparse beard, like the others. His chin-length hair was disheveled. The sleeves of his white blouse were rolled up, revealing muscled forearms. Yoshiko noticed the blue veins popping out.

He was looking at her as if he expected an answer.

"Why not Mary Cassatt?" she asked with a smile.

Four years later they were together on a steamer bound for Europe.

"Paris is the center of the art world," gushed the young man, whose name was Taizo. "The Japanese art establishment is too conservative. Moribund. If we want to create something new and alive, we must be among progressive thinkers."

Already, as they sailed out of Yokohama, Taizo was scheming as to how he'd meet the great French artists. Yoshiko sat on the deck, gathering images in her sketchbook—the vultures at the Parsi Towers of Silence, the young boys selling ostrich feathers in Aden, the purple hills of Egypt. She made a study of camels and Bedouins spotted from the Suez Canal.

Finally in Paris, they settled into a cold water flat in the shadow of Sacré Coeur. Broke, and longing for rice and green tea, they subsisted on day-old bread and syrupy coffee. And they painted.

One afternoon, Taizo returned home from a visit to a café with another artist in tow. A Frenchman.

"This is Jean-Claude," Taizo said. "I've told him you would sit for him." Whiskey wafted on his breath.

Yoshiko bowed, unable to muster a smile.

The Frenchman caught her hand in his and brought it to his lips. She did not like the scratching of his whiskers on her skin.

"*Enchanté, madame.*"

Yoshiko said nothing.

That evening over bowls of burnt stew, she exploded. "What about my art? When can I paint if I have to sit on a chair all day?"

Taizo scooped a mouthful of stew. His jaws worked on the tough meat, the cheapest at the market.

"It's just for one painting," he pleaded. "We are so poor right now. Later we will drink champagne and dance in the fountains. I'll buy you silk parasols and a new kimono. We'll have parties…"

He was floating away on his fantasies, but then he caught sight of his wife's grim mouth. "Please," he said, taking up her hands. "I beg of you. Just this once."

As the months went by, it seemed as if Yoshiko was modeling more and more, while Taizo was painting less and less. "The French are wild about Japan," he said. "Everyone's painting Japanese vases, fans, kimono. And of course, they want to paint our women."

Taizo, on the other hand, wanted to paint *les francaises*. He stayed out till all hours drinking at the feet of the can-can girls, commiserating with compatriots, and then sleeping till noon.

Meanwhile, Yoshiko rose at dawn and began mixing colors. She stayed at her easel until Taizo stirred and then she hid her work under a sheet. As he sipped his morning café before heading off to his studio, he was usually too bleary to notice the paint stains on his wife's hands.

And then one afternoon, around the time of day that Taizo was usually in his studio, he returned to find Yoshiko with a brush in her hand. She moved to block her easel and the beginnings of a garden. But Taizo didn't even seem to notice. He was holding a bottle of champagne—the expensive kind. Already his face was a deep red from drinking.

"*Ma petite*," he said, spinning into the room. "*On va celebrer*."

Yoshiko frowned at his atrocious accent. "What is there to celebrate?" she asked, rising with hands on hips. That bottle was worth three sittings for Jean-Claude, money better spent on meat and bread.

"I've sold a painting to the Countess. Maybe two or three."

The Countess was famous. Even Yoshiko, who never went to the cafés and cabarets, had heard of her. She was known not only for her exotic pets and scandalous liaisons (husbands, scoundrels, a woman or two), but also for her patronage of the arts. Rumor had it that she'd saved more than one poet from starvation or suicide. And she was a trendsetter. If the Countess showed interest in an artist, others soon did, too.

Taizo started spending more time at home. He wanted to bring potential patrons around for authentic Japanese meals. The French interest in Japan went beyond art and Taizo was exploiting it for all it was worth.

Suddenly, Yoshiko was down on her knees with a whisk and a bowl, performing tea ceremony, twice a day. When she might have been working on her own art, she was sweeping out corners and packing rice balls in her palms.

But things were better. They could afford a new loaf of bread and cheese and fresh fruit every day. The meat in the pot was tender. They indulged in flaky tarts from *la pâtisserie* down the street.

That is, until the morning Taizo woke up coughing. Blood spattered the white sheets. Yoshiko lost herself for a moment in the crimson patterns before a new dawning caused her stomach to wrench.

"Tuberculosis," the bearded doctor said.

Taizo was admitted to a ward for the contagious, a dark corner in an otherwise lively hospital.

When Yoshiko arrived each morning with a basket of oranges and rice balls, she held a handkerchief pressed to her nose and mouth. She kept it there for the length of the visit and didn't dare to touch him.

In the afternoons, she went from gallery to gallery, selling his finished paintings. A few incomplete canvases were propped against the wall having been temporarily abandoned for commissioned portraits of daughters and lap dogs.

When Taizo returned home, he was only well enough to paint for an hour or two a day before collapsing in fatigue. Yoshiko helped him back into bed then sat at the table, head in hands, listening to the breath rattle in his chest. They were doomed, she thought. She would never be able to go back to Japan.

Snow swirled outside the window. She shivered and rose to make a pot of tea. Seeing a bottle of whiskey on the shelf, she changed her mind.

The first sip made her shudder. The second made her cough. By the third swallow, her limbs were beginning to heat up. Suddenly, the snow and the sleeping husband and the empty purse no longer seemed so severe.

And then she bent over the chamber pot and threw up.

As she huddled on the floor, dabbing at her brow, she caught sight of a landscape Taizo had left undone. The trees standing alone made her feel desolate. She would add human figures.

The next afternoon, while her husband snored, she brought out her easel and palette and began mixing color. Taizo had a particular technique, a fondness for gouache and thick impasto. She experimented on bits of cloth until she had a close approximation.

Finally, she turned to her husband's canvas, brush poised in the air. Her heart galloped wildly. What if she ruined it? What if she couldn't sell it? She thought of the francs rattling in the coffee can. What if she could?

With a deep breath she began to work. As she became more and more engrossed, she forgot her violation. The pure joy of creation filled her. She didn't even notice when it stopped snowing.

By the time she finished, it was dark. Taizo was just waking up. He would need his supper. She set the canvas aside to dry and covered her easel with a worn sheet.

She let the finished painting sit there for a few days, a little afraid of what she was planning to do next. But when the pantry was bare, but for a few rat droppings, and there was no longer enough money to pay the next month's rent, she took a deep breath and rolled up the canvas.

"Where are you going?" Taizo's weak voice rose from the bed.

"For a promenade," she said, and left before he could ask any more questions.

She walked along the icy streets, trying to ignore the wind biting her face. Twice, she slipped and fell. By the time she arrived at the Countess's door, her fingers, though gloved, were stiff with cold. She stamped her feet to warm them and pressed the bell.

A maid appeared almost immediately. The white apron she wore over her black uniform was crisp and spotless. Yoshiko couldn't believe she did any housework at all. Maybe her job was simply answering the door.

"I'm here to show the Countess a painting," she said.

The maid nodded and motioned her inside.

As Yoshiko fumbled in her purse for a calling card, the rolled-up canvas escaped her thawing fingers and fell to the floor. Yoshiko gasped, but the other woman remained impassive.

"I'll tell the mistress that you are here." She disappeared, carrying Taizo's card on her tray.

While she waited, Yoshiko took in the high ceilings, the vivid Turkish carpets, and the ornate, gilded sconces on the walls. Such grandeur, she thought. If worse came to worst, maybe she could ask the Countess to take her on as a servant.

She was lost in a daydream of herself, warm and fed, flicking a feather duster over the frames of the paintings the lady had collected, when the Countess herself strolled into the room, a spider monkey perched on her shoulder. She struck a pose a few feet from Yoshiko, one hand cocked on her hip, the other flourishing a cigarette in a long black holder.

The woman looked Yoshiko up and down, lips curved into a faint smile. "So how is my dear little Taizo?" she asked, her voice a deep purr. "I haven't seen him around lately."

Yoshiko fought back a ripple of revulsion. "He's very well, thank you. He's working hard."

"*Ah, bon.* I am happy to hear that." She turned back down the hallway. "Come along then. Show me what you've got." Yoshiko trailed behind.

In the parlor, the walls of which were hung with a profusion of paintings in clashing styles and colors, Yoshiko unfurled her ware. The Countess spread it across a red velvet hassock and examined it from all angles. Her gaze danced over Yoshiko's work. She seemed not to notice that parts of the painting were done by a different hand. From time to time she puffed on her cigarette, then exhaled rings of smoke. Yoshiko tried hard not to cough.

After what seemed like a month, the Countess finally looked her in the eye and said, "I like it. I'll buy it."

Yoshiko managed to get a good price for the painting. They'd be able to eat for another month or two. In the meantime, she would work on the other unfinished canvases she'd found.

No one seemed to notice Yoshiko's additions, not even Taizo, who was oblivious to the disappearing paintings. Dealers continued to praise Taizo's work. Money once again flowed into their home.

And then one morning, Yoshiko woke to find her husband stiff and cold. All of his paintings had been sold or bartered. Yoshiko was alone in Paris without a sou.

Now, standing before the last work in the gallery, Yoshiko tries hard not to think about the days spent begging at her husband's patrons' doors. She wills away the memory of her hollow stomach and the tears in the soles of her shoes.

The painting is titled "Woman, Blossoming." The date puts it at the year of Taizo's death. It shows a woman, Yoshiko, in the full flower of her beauty. But she is not like the demure Oriental odalisques of other great artists. She does not gaze wistfully off to the side while holding a fan, but straight at the viewer. She is not restricted by a cocoon-tight kimono; hers drapes loosely over her shoulders and pools on the floor.

"This is one of his best," a goateed grey-haired man says, leaning in close to examine the brushwork. "Here, he returns to the theme of his native country, but with a twist."

His companion complies. "Yes, this is so much better than that famous one of the can-can girls. There is such vitality here. It's as if she were about to step down from the wall."

"There's no telling what Taizo would have done had he lived longer."

The two men cast a glance at the signature in the corner of the painting and move on to the table where tea and cakes are being served.

Yoshiko remains, a Mona Lisa smile on her lips. She remembers being back in that Parisian apartment sitting before a blank canvas. She took a long look at herself in the mirror, the pink kimono loose around her shoulders, and then she dipped her brush in color and began to paint.

The Rain in Katoomba

The Rain in Katoomba

*U*sually Takako Soga took her little Pomeranian along on her daily constitutional, but on this afternoon, a light rain was falling. After frying up some strips of beef and serving them into the dog's silver dish with chopsticks, she would set out alone.

She had never pampered herself in the way that she did her pet, and this, she believed, explained why she was so tough. At the age of eighty, her white hair had grown sparse and her skin hung loosely on the bones, but she could still walk longer and farther than her nineteen-year-old granddaughter.

Her granddaughter—what was her name? Oh, Aya. Sometimes it was easier to remember the people and places of long ago than those she encountered every day. Her granddaughter Aya could hardly walk a hundred meters in those spiky heels she always wore. Then again, she didn't need to walk. Her boyfriend, a restaurant dishwasher with dyed blond hair, drove her anywhere she wanted to go in his jacked-up sports car. The horn played a melody—some old American folk song.

Aya was probably out with him now. She'd breezed in a couple hours before, having finished her classes at the university, changed her clothes, and gone out again.

Takako and her dog were alone in the house. Her son and his wife were at work and wouldn't be home till later. There was no need to leave a note. Everyone knew her routine, and besides, she'd be back before anyone returned.

She put an orange in her pocket, intending to make an offering at her husband's grave on the way home, then stepped out the door, leaving her umbrella behind. Sometimes she walked along the sea wall, in view of the surfers and fishing trawls, but today she chose to amble through the patchwork of wooden houses and farmers' paddies.

Raindrops dimpled the rice fields where the first green shoots of the season were rising from the water. No guardrails or fences separated the flooded paddies from the narrow road. Once, Takako had seen a foreigner on a bicycle veer off into a patch of lotus roots. She had struggled to contain her laughter when he'd emerged, confused and muddy.

The rain fell, dappling her cotton housedress. It was a gentle rain, almost like a mist—like the blue mist that rose from the gum trees in Katoomba.

It had been raining like this on the day, just after the war, when she opened her door and saw the tall, ginger-haired solider in green fatigues.

"Paul," she said, her voice barely a whisper.

She had not seen this man in years, not since she'd lived in Australia with her father, but she hadn't forgotten those agate eyes.

He took off his hat at the sight of her in a raggedy silk kimono. The last time he'd seen her, she'd been wearing floral cotton. Her hair had been thick and lustrous then, falling down her back.

Her father, sitting behind her in a gloomy corner of the house, did not recognize the visitor. Takako knew that the war had unravelled her father's mind. He cowered in the presence of the occupying forces. When he saw the pale giants patrolling the streets, he ducked into alleys. Takako knew he expected bayonets and bombs, but this soldier handed her a bag of rice and some cans of beef and chicken.

"Come in," she said. "Have supper with us."

She set a kettle to boil, then poured hot water over the tea leaves she'd already used three times that day. He stood among her children and tried to tease a few words of English from her father, but the old man remained mute.

"Is he going to kill us?" the eldest boy asked in Japanese.

Takako presented Paul with a cup of tea on a tray and frowned at her son. "What a question! No, of course not. The fighting is over. He's an old friend."

And then she turned from the boy to the soldier and switched to English. "How did you find me?"

He patted his chest pocket and drew out an envelope. It was torn and wrinkled, slightly yellowed with age. The ink had faded, but she recognized her handwriting and the Japanese stamp.

She looked away, embarrassed, and waited for him to put the envelope back in his pocket.

"Your husband?"

"Alive," she said quickly. "He's away, looking for work." She wondered what Paul would have said if she'd been widowed, but she quickly banished the thought. Her husband was a good man, though quiet and sometimes stern. She hadn't married him for love. Even so, over the years a bond had formed between them. She had cried the day he went off to war. Now he was back, a broken man, but perhaps he would mend.

"Your wife?" she asked, turning to Paul. She was sure that he, too, had married.

"Back in Sydney," he said. "With our two sons." He reached into another pocket and withdrew a photo of two fat-cheeked lads with carrot-colored hair.

When supper was ready, Takako, her children, her father and their guest gathered on their knees around the low table and ate slowly. They tried to believe that there would be food on the table the next day, too. No one complained that the soup was watery or the beef stringy. Every bite was a feast in itself.

After they'd eaten enough to quiet their rumbling stomachs, Paul entertained the children with magic tricks. He pulled chocolate bars from behind their ears, made sticks of gum appear in his empty palm. He regaled them with a song, something about a waltzing Matilda, which Takako remembered from long ago, and danced with an exaggerated swinging of arms and a side-to-side shuffle. His slapstick manner made her laugh. Her skinny children whooped and hollered for the first time in months.

For one brief moment, she forgot about the bombs, the hunger, the kimonos and precious lacquerware sold on the black market, and she wanted to kiss him. She felt the urge to bury her face in that broad chest. But then she thought of her husband, our searching for work till he was too tired to sleep, and she asked the soldier to leave.

He was from Katoomba.

"Katoomba," she said to herself now, remembering. What a long time ago that was. (What year? 1940? 1941? It was so hard to keep things straight. Time seemed so slippery now.) She had gone with her father to Australia in search of a tribe of men who wore bones through their noses. Her father was, at the time, consumed by an interest in anthropology, and the desire to find these men kept him awake at night. But the truth is, he was a dilettante. On the edge of the desert, he learned about the artists who gathered in the Blue Mountains of eastern Australia. Intrigued, he abandoned his quest and went off to join them, even though he had never painted before.

There were a lot of them in the Blue Mountains. Sometimes they set up their easels at the edge of the gorge and painted the Three Sisters, a spectacular rock formation carved by wind, rain, and time. There was one woman who always wore a picture hat and arranged her palette at Echo Point, in full view of the valley, but only painted bowls of fruit. Takako had once been invited to a Frenchman's studio to pose as Joan of Arc, but she'd fled when he'd asked her to take off her clothes. Then there were the naturalists who spent hours on the details of one leaf of a fern, and her father, of course, who painted the cliffs.

Takako roamed the little town filled with Victorian houses with gingerbread trim. She'd been quite free then. Her mother had died when she was small. Her father was too distracted to care what she did. He didn't notice when she began to bloom beneath her cotton dress.

Although she was no judge of art and preferred nature itself to oil and canvas renderings, she suspected that her father lacked talent. He had sold no paintings. Worse, he had racked up quite a tab at the bar and haberdashery and, having taught mah-jongg to a few local men, now had gambling debts as well. She suspected that he was planning on trading in on their aristocratic forebears: he'd lure a rich son-in-law with his daughter's pedigree. But who cared about such a thing in the Blue Mountains of Australia?

Takako wrote to her grandfather in Kyoto asking for money. At first, she'd signed her father's name, but sympathies for the wayward son had quickly run out. Now she appealed in her own voice. She wrote that her kimono was torn and she had no other (although she now wore cotton dresses like the Australian girls). She wrote that she and her father were subsisting on mealy rice. One day, during the war, these things would be true, but not yet.

Takako was at the post office mailing a letter to her grandfather on the day that she first saw Paul. She'd stepped into the one-room office and almost bumped into a young man on his way out. He was tall enough to lose his head in the clouds, she thought. And skinny. She knew how to make lamb stew, having been taught by a neighbor, and she thought she could fatten him up.

"Oh, excuse me," she said, raising her eyes instead of lowering them.

His chin was dimpled and speckled with reddish whiskers. His Adam's apple bobbed when he swallowed. He steadied her by the shoulders. "Are you all right?"

"Yes," she said. "Are you?"

He laughed then, as if he found it funny that such a twig of a girl might be worried about having caused harm to a man who loomed like a tree. He laughed, Takako thought, like a kookaburra.

After she'd posted her letter, she found him outside, waiting for her.

She knew—before he spoke another word, before he asked her to walk with him, before he invited her to join him for English tea—that she would fall in love with him.

Her father never looked at her, hardly ever spoke to her except to demand meals and hot bathwater and clean brushes for painting, but this tall young man with wavy, ginger hair stared at her until she blushed.

"I've never seen you before," he said. "Have you been here long?"

She explained that she'd come from Japan to Katoomba only a few months before.

She had never learned the arts of flower arrangement or tea ceremony or how to fold a fan like other young women of her station, but her English was perfect. In solitary times, of which there were many, she read books borrowed from the library.

Paul was a student of another kind. He attended the university beyond Leura, Bullaburra, and Warrimoo. He had come all the way from Sydney, where he was studying to be a geology teacher. He knew all of the stories about the Three Sisters, both scientific and aboriginal, and he chose to tell her the latter.

"Once upon a time," he began, "there was a witch doctor who had three daughters of extraordinary beauty. Their names were Meenhi, Wimlah, and Gunnedoo. One day the girls were playing at the edge of a cliff while their father was in the valley hunting for food. Meenhi threw a stone at a centipede, but she missed, and the stone went over the cliff. Now, one of the laws of the bush is that you must never throw a stone from a cliff. It brings bad luck.

"The falling stone woke the Bunyip, a mythical creature of the bush. Furious that his sleep had been interrupted, he lumbered toward them, making a terrible noise. The witch doctor heard the commotion and rushed toward his daughters to save them, but he was too far away to reach them in time. He pointed his magic bone at them and turned them into stone. The Bunyip crashed into the daughters, who were now rock. He became very angry and so he pursued the witch doctor, who turned himself into a lyrebird and ran into a cave. He dropped his magic bone in the process so he couldn't change himself back into his human form nor free his daughters from the stone."

Paul told her that the witch doctor was still searching for his bone, and had been searching for hundreds of years. Takako was jealous. She knew that her father would never go to such trouble to try to save her. He would give up searching right away and head to the bar for a glass of whiskey.

Paul invited Takako to a small cafe with a view of the valley. They sat over china cups of Earl Grey tea, nibbling biscuits imported from England. He wanted to know all about Japan. "Tell me about the volcanoes," he said, looking deeply into her eyes.

Takako knew no such stories, but of Mount Fuji she told him, "It's the most beautiful mountain in all the world," although had had never seen it.

They began taking bush walks together. Takako saw a koala hugging a tree at high noon. Following Paul, she waded through ferns and listened to cockatoos calling her name. Gradually, their conversations shifted from discussions of plate tectonics to wildflowers. They spoke of poetry and yearnings of the heart.

One afternoon, while bent in admiration of a mountain devil, a spiky red flower peculiar to that region, she turned to see Paul looking at her. She rose slowly, meeting his gaze, and stood like one of the Three Sisters, waiting to see what would happen next.

Paul rested his freckled hands on her shoulders, lowered his face, and gave her the first kiss of her life.

That evening, Takako sat across from her father at the dinner table in a delighted daze. She kept stirring and stirring and stirring the soup, but she did not eat. From time to time, she brought her fingertips to her lips. Her father slurped in oblivion.

"*Otoosan*," she said at last. "Tell me. How did you meet my mother?"

He dropped his spoon, and it rattled in the china dish. "Meet? My mother and father picked her out. She was recommended by some matchmaker. She was pretty enough, your mother, but weak. I wish they'd have found someone sturdier for me to marry."

Takako tried to conceal her disappointment. She'd been hoping for more of a story—a romance, in fact, like those in the books she'd been borrowing from the library.

Her father looked up then and squinted at her. "She looked a lot like you do now. How old are you anyway?"

"Twenty."

He frowned. "Maybe we'd better start thinking about finding a husband for you."

Takako almost told him about Paul and the kiss in the bush, but then she thought better of it. He hadn't ever fallen in love himself. He would never understand her feelings.

And then there was the day when Paul and Takako stood at Echo Point and he hurled her name into the valley: "Takako-ko-ko. Will you marry me-me-me?"

Giddy, she had shouted back, "Yes-ess-ess."

When their voices had faded, Paul turned to her and took both of her hands in his. "I want to do this properly," he said. "I'm going to finish my studies, find a good job, and then I'll ask your father for your hand in marriage. I couldn't ask him now, without any means of supporting you."

Takako wanted to laugh. Her father had no means himself. They were living on the good graces of the towns-people. That, and money sent from Kyoto.

Paul did not have a diamond ring to give her, but he tied a blade of grass around her finger as a symbol of their promise. And then he kissed her and walked with her as far as she would permit.

She didn't want him to meet her father, not quite yet. Paul was her secret, her life apart from him.

On this evening, she decided that she wouldn't go home at all. She would wander under the stars, considering her impending freedom. She wouldn't have to scrub the paint splatters from her father's shirts or fetch him tea. She would no longer have to write letters to Kyoto. He could fend for himself.

She didn't know then that there would be rumors of war, that her father would drag her back to Japan, that she would spend her days in a garden behind a stone wall. She would write long letters to Paul, but they would go unanswered. Or perhaps the replies were intercepted. Later, she would wonder who threw the stone from the cliff causing so much bad luck, but on this night, such a future was unimaginable.

Takako knew that her father and hsi friends were playing mah-jongg at the kitchen table, clicking the tiles against wood. She did not go back. She continued her midnight stroll even when a light rain began to fall. Her cotton dress damp-ened, but she didn't care. She was warm with love. Dizzy with it. She started twirling and twirling because she could not contain her joy. She twirled until she fell, breathless, into the mud, and even then she didn't care that she had soiled her clothing. She just sat there, feeling the rain on her upturned face.

After awhile, the eastern sky turned pink, and she found herself face to face with a young Japanese man wearing a white coat. A car was parked on the road beyond. An ambulance.

"Are you all right, *obaachan*? Do you know who you are?"

"Of course," she said. "I am Takako."

The young man looked relieved.

Takako tried to get up out of the mud, but her limbs were too stiff. The stranger reached under her arms and helped her stand. Mud and cold water dragged at her hem.

"Do you have any idea how you came to be sitting in this rice field?" the man asked.

Takako was confused. She suddenly felt a chill.

Someone put a blanket over her shoulders, and she was lifted onto a stretcher.

Another man with glasses and streaks of white in his hair approached. This one's face was oddly familiar, though she couldn't think of his name.

"*Okaasan*," he said, "we've been worried sick. The volunteer fire department has been up all night looking for you. How in the world did you get so far from home?"

He had called her "mother." This was her son, then, though how could that be? She was only twenty and newly engaged.

The man jiggled her shoulder gently, as if trying to get her attention. "Do you have any idea where you are?"

At this, Takako smiled and looked up into his face. "Yes,"

she said. She closed her eyes and saw the blue mists rising in front of her. "I'm in Katoomba."

Driving

Driving

Yvonne Hamada saw the cement mixer turn onto the narrow bridge, saw that it was coming straight at them, picking up speed as it rolled. She knew that Ryu's sedan was no match for that monster on wheels. There was hardly enough room for one car, let alone two; these roads had been built for cracker box-sized economy cars, not the all-terrain vehicles and American-sized dump trucks of '90's Japan.

Ryu let up on the accelerator ever so slightly.

Next to him, Yvonne closed her eyes, shrank back against the passenger seat—"the death seat," her brother had always called it. "This is it," she whispered. "I hope someone knows enough English to notify my parents in the States."

But then the car swayed as the truck whooshed past—within inches, no doubt—and Yvonne opened her eyes.

They were safe. There were no other cars ahead of them. To her left, she could see jet skiers speeding over the river.

On the opposite shore, boys cast their lines, as they did on any other Sunday afternoon.

Out of the corner of her eye, she could see Ryu's dark head leaning sideways as he fiddled with the radio dial in search of baseball. The car swerved toward the guardrail. This, just after they'd narrowly escaped death by two-ton truck.

"Ryu? Honey?" she said, her voice high and tight. "Do you mind looking at where you're going?"

He glanced at her instead, frowned, and then turned back to the road. "If you don't like my driving, you can drive."

Yvonne did not want to drive and she decided that she wouldn't make another sound. She saw the traffic signal a few meters ahead turn yellow and she figured that Ryu would race through the red light as usual. She decided that for once she would hold her tongue, but then the car slowed and came to a stop. Yvonne smiled at her reformed husband.

He looked at her, saw the grin, then began fussing with the radio again and didn't notice when the light changed.

Yvonne immediately forgot her vow of silence. "Sweetie? It's green. You can go now."

Ryu gripped the steering wheel once again. "*Ao*," he said, a smile playing at the corners of his mouth.

"It's not blue. *Green*. Just look at that light. How can you call that color blue?"

Ryu shrugged as they crossed the intersection. They'd had this exchange many times before. It was so familiar as to be comfortable to Yvonne. She settled back in her seat, finally content to enjoy the ride.

Back in the States, Yvonne had cruised around in a banana-yellow hatchback, but since coming to Japan ten years ago to teach English in the countryside of Shikoku, she didn't drive at all. Well, there had been that one time. Before she'd met Ryu, a Japanese suitor had rented a little red convertible as a surprise. Yvonne remembered the salty wind whipping her long blonde hair, the sight of the waves breaking on the shore, and then her date's absolute terror when she took a turn down the wrong side of the road. She was scared, too, when she nearly sideswiped a stop sign, having misjudged the distance between the side of the car and the edge of the road. Since then, Yvonne usually relied on public transportation or her mountain bike. Sometimes she allowed Ryu to drive her, though these days she preferred to stay in their recently mortgaged home where she knew that she was safe and in no danger of breaking the law.

In Japan, Driver's Ed wasn't a school subject as it was in the States. Would-be drivers enrolled in private driving schools where a series of lessons cost as much as a year at Yvonne's university. Not only was it expensive, but also inconvenient as students had to sign up for lessons on a first-come first-serve basis, with everyone vying for the same time slots.

There were actually a lot of adults in Japan who didn't know how to drive. Her mother-in-law, Mrs. Hamada, for instance. She tooled around on a bright blue 50cc scooter. It was enough to get her to the hospital where she worked as a cook or to the store for groceries. For journeys to more distant places, her husband would drive.

"You don't need a license," he told her. "I'll take you wherever you want to go."

Lying awake in bed one night, Ryu said, "I think my mother is going to divorce my father."

"What?" Yvonne turned to Ryu and tried to make out his

expression in the dark. Was he serious? Divorce was a Western obsession. Here, women made do. They endured; they persevered.

"She said that she can't talk to my father anymore. He just drinks and plays Go."

Yvonne thought that maybe being married to an American made him see divorce as an option. She was always trying to explain her complicated family relations—half-cousins, stepfathers, adoptees, and so on.

"If my mother leaves my father, can she live with us?" Ryu propped himself on his elbows so he could look down at her moon-bathed face. "You two get along well. I think it would work out, don't you?"

Yvonne's limbs froze. She mumbled unintelligibly, trying to quell the sudden panic. Why not say yes? It would never happen, she thought. Mrs. Hamada would never ask for a divorce.

"Yvonne?"

"Sure, whatever," she said.

Ryu leaned down and kissed her, then fell back against the pillow. Seemingly content, he rolled over and began to snore softly almost immediately.

Yvonne tossed and turned until dawn. Before they'd married, Yvonne had paid close attention to how Ryu treated his mother. She'd always believed that men who were kind and considerate to the women who'd raised them would be the same way toward their wives. At family dinners, Ryu took his mother's side in arguments with his father. When the meal had ended, Ryu helped clear away the dishes, just as he did now at home. And he always spoke of his mother with words like "strong," "patient," and "brave."

When Ryu had asked her to marry him, Yvonne had

made sure that they wouldn't be living with his parents. It wouldn't be good for their relationship, her friends and relatives had warned. Her grandmother had blamed her own divorce on an overbearing German live-in mother-in-law.

Early on in their relationship, Ryu and Yvonne had talked about living abroad—maybe in a third country that would be foreign to both of them. They had first drawn together by mutual cultural curiosity—Yvonne's interest in traditional Japan arts, and Ryu's love of American freedom, frankness and Major League baseball—and by a passion for travel.

Sometimes, as they lay together in bed just before sleep, they talked about the places that they would visit—the jungles of Borneo, the cobblestoned streets of Avignon. Yvonne was hungry for that initial burst of wonder she'd felt on first arriving in Japan. The novelty had long since worn off, and she was in need of a new fix. Ryu's job, however, kept him busy most of the year. The economy was failing, and he couldn't risk taking a vacation for awhile. So far, most of the trips they'd planned were just wishes.

Yvonne remembered the first time Ryu's parents came to check out their new house—before they'd even decided to buy it.

They had discovered the place by chance—a two story dwelling less than a kilometer away from the cramped apartment they'd been renting. It was a boxy, Western-style prefab construction with stucco walls—not especially beautiful, but Yvonne couldn't wait to move in. They'd spent the first two years of their marriage breathing down each other's necks. They were ready for wide rooms filled with sunlight, a yard big enough for barbecues. Friends thought that they were being greedy—just the two of them moving into a house previously inhabited by a family of six—but Yvonne's American soul needed space and solitude.

The only problem with the house was the driveway, which was steep, narrow and bordered by a cement wall. Ryu's father had parked on the street, not bothering with the challenge.

"So this is where you want to live," Ryu's father said as he wandered the empty rooms, his slippers scuffing on the hardwood floors. "There's only one room with tatami mats. There is no alcove for hanging scrolls."

His own house was a Japanese-style structure of weathered wood, with a rock garden out front. The rooms were separated by sliding doors, and the windows were hidden behind paper screens.

Mrs. Hamada trailed behind, a smile hiding her disappointment. "I was hoping we'd all live together," she nearly whimpered. "We added on last year…"

Yvonne knew about the twelve-mat room that had been adjoined to their house. She'd thought at the time that it was for Ryu's sister, who stayed there in the later stages of her two pregnancies. Now, she realized that in spite of their son's international marriage and his Western-style outspokenness, they still had hopes that he'd turn out traditional.

"We'll be nearby," Yvonne said. "It's only a fifteen minute drive." She meant to remind them—Ryu, his parents, everyone—that her own family was thousands of miles away. That in agreeing to buy this house, rooting herself so near Ryu's birthplace, she was making concessions of her own. The dream of a life in Bali/Paris/Sydney was becoming dimmer and dimmer.

Mr. Hamada had agreed to lend the couple money for a down payment on the house. They took out a bank loan for the rest. Yvonne and Ryu had furnished the house with leather sofas and oak tables, Georgia O'Keefe prints for the walls. They hung curtains in the windows. Yvonne had planted tulips and irises in the garden.

The day after the "divorce conversation," Yvonne was in the kitchen working on a new concoction—a Thai dish involving lots of chilies. She had a CD playing, the music cranked up loud, and she danced while she chopped lemon grass.

She didn't hear the front door open.

"*Konnichiwa!*"

Yvonne jumped, nearly slicing her finger. She turned to find Ryu's mother right behind her. Her permanent was smashed down from wearing a helmet. Obviously, she'd come on her scooter. She was smiling broadly, flashing her gold teeth. She held a cloth bundle in one hand, lofted it in the air to show what she'd brought.

Yvonne rushed over to the CD player to turn down the volume. She was suddenly conscious of the laundry piled on a chair, the mail stacked on the table, the unwashed dishes in the sink. Her scalp prickled with irritation. Why hadn't Mrs. Hamada called first? Why hadn't she locked the door?

In the now quiet room, she shoved a cook book aside and motioned for her mother-in-law to sit.

"I'll make you some tea," she said, setting a kettle of water to boil.

Mrs. Hamada settled in a chair. She began riffling absentmindedly through the letters and bills on the table.

"No, no, that's not necessary," she said.

"Please. I'd like a cup myself," Yvonne insisted. She wanted to order her mother-in-law to leave the mail alone, but it was mostly in English. She couldn't read it anyway.

"I don't want to trouble you."

Yvonne opened a canister and shook tea leaves into the tea pot. She was mostly a coffee drinker. The porcelain teapot, painted with chrysanthemums on its side, only came out of the cupboard for guests.

"It's no trouble," she said.

"Well, if you're having some…"

Yvonne turned away and rolled her eyes. Sometimes she got fed up with the verbal dance. She knew that if she didn't offer tea, her mother-in-law would think her rude. And she knew that Ryu's mother was a master of beating around the bush, exceptionally skilled at indirect response. She would have to invite her to stay for dinner too.

As she poured hot water over tea leaves, she remembered Ryu's words of the night before. What if he was right? What if she really would rather live with her son than her husband? Hadn't she raised him to adore her? Hadn't she poured all of her efforts into making sure that he would never leave her?

She cast a glance at her abandoned culinary project. If Ryu's mother moved in with them, they'd have to forget about trying exotic new dishes. Ryu's parents lived on a strict diet of fish, rice and miso soup. She'd once found the remains of a casserole she'd sent over in the trash of her in-laws' kitchen.

In the afternoons, when she came home from work, she wouldn't be able to settle in a chair with a book. She'd have to drink tea with her mother-in-law. They'd never be able to go on the trips that she and Ryu had imagined taking. Could she imagine Mrs. Hamada on a bus in Mumbai? No, way.

And they would be forced to speak in Japanese all the time. This house, this former haven, would be an extension of the foreign world beyond its walls. Yvonne needed one place—just one—where she didn't have to worry about committing cultural blunders, where she could be wholly herself.

She brought the teapot and teacups on a tray to the table where her mother-in-law sat waiting. Normally, she wouldn't have bothered with the lacquer tray, but with a guest present, decorum was required. The two of them sat together sipping the hot tea. The room was silent except for the sound of Ryu's mother's slurping.

A month later, Mr. Hamada bid his wife good-bye as she hopped on her scooter for work. He read the newspaper, poured himself a second cup of tea, and got dressed. Sunshine was blessing all of the flowers and plants and tiny trees in his garden. He felt the warm rays on his taut-skinned face when he stepped outside. He bent to run his hands lightly over the leaves of a peppermint plant then sniffed at his fingers. Scent of gum. Then he began tugging at the weeds that had sprung up and tossing them into a pile at the center of the yard.

He went into the shed and took the trimming shears from their hook, began snipping at twigs, giving the bushes form. He worked with total concentration. When the pain shot through his arm and chest, he dropped the shears and grabbed at his heart. That evening his wife found him staring at a bush with a look of surprise.

At least that's how Yvonne imagined it all. Heart attack. *Shinzo mahi.* It sounded like a Hawaiian fish, something you could order from a menu: "I'll have the *shinzo mahi* and a glass of white wine."

As she ironed her black dress, preparing for the funeral, inappropriate thoughts kept popping into her brain. She wasn't sure what she was feeling. Sadness, sure, but underneath, panic was waiting to grab her by the throat. Mrs.

Hamada was now alone. There was no need to even consider divorce.

The morning of the funeral, relatives from afar arrived at Mrs. Hamada's house. Yvonne had met them at her wedding to Ryu, four years before, but she didn't remember their faces or their names.

Yvonne waited in the kitchen, prepared for duty. Ryu brushed by her as if she were a stranger. He hovered at his mother's elbow, urging her to sit, to rest, to drink something. To Yvonne: "The priest is coming soon. Prepare the tray."

Yvonne felt that everyone was were watching her, the only foreigner in the house. Would she sit with her legs sprawled open? Would she laugh and flap her arms around like a duck? Would she be like those Americans they'd seen on TV? She bowed to each aunt, uncle, cousin, neighbor who came to the door. She ushered them to the room where her father-in-law's body lay in a pine box. She brought them tea on a tray, set the cup down on the tatami floor near them with two hands.

Back in the kitchen, she hunched over the too-low sink and washed the teacups. Cousin Kanako joined her. "So will you live here from now on?"

Yvonne looked into the cousin's face. She was fortyish, earnest-looking, with bobbed hair hooked behind her ears.

"I can't," she whispered. "In America..."

"But this is Japan. You can't just leave her alone in this big house. She'll have nothing to look forward to." Kanako leaned in closer. "I live with my mother-in-law. It's not so bad. We do embroidery together."

Yvonne shuddered, but Kanako didn't seem to notice. She should have been thinking about Mr. Hamada reminiscing, perhaps, about the freshwater pearl necklace he had once brought her from Kyoto. Or the time he had tried to teach her how to play Go—the arrangement of black and white disks on the playing board. Or the time the four of them Mr. and Mrs. Hamada, Ryu and Yvonne, had gone to a karaoke club and sung *enka* together. Instead, Yvonne could only think about herself. She could feel her future closing in on her like the lid of a box. It was getting harder and harder to breathe.

"Yvonne, the priest is here now." An aunt appeared to give directions. "Bring him the tray."

Yvonne shuffled in her slippers down the hallway to the tatami room. The black-clad relatives knelt in rows, prayer beads twined around their fingers. One of the aunts was sobbing loudly.

The young priest nodded slightly as Yvonne set down a tea cup before him. He tugged back the sleeve of his white kimono, and took a sip. When he had finished, Yvonne returned the cup to the kitchen and joined the mourners at the back of the room.

The priest began chanting.

Yvonne fixed her eyes on the small of the back of the uncle sitting in front of her, and tried not to squirm as all of the feeling went out of her legs. She didn't understand a word that the priest was saying.

Later in the day, after Mr. Hamada's remains had been cremated, and it was just Ryu, Yvonne and Mrs. Hamada in the kitchen, the older woman turned to her daughter-in-law.

"Everyone said that you are a good bride," she said. "Not many young women know how to serve tea."

And then she saw the rest of her life as a succession of teacups. She'd fill them, place them before guests, and wash them, and this would go on and on and on. Every time one of Mrs. Hamada's friends or neighbors came to visit, she would be forced into this role.

"It's better to establish yourself as a bad daughter-in-law," her Japanese friend Maya had once told her. Now she understood.

"Mother," Ryu said. He sounded tired, yet gentle. "We want you to live with us."

Yvonne could not move. Her head was becoming light.

"No, no, no. I can't leave this house. Your father and I lived here together for many years."

"He's dead now. It's time to move on."

Yvonne was stunned. Mr. Hamada's ashes had not yet cooled, and his son was already smothering the memory of him. He was already thinking of a new life where Yvonne would sit at the table in silence while the two of them rattled away in their language.

"Then we will move in here," Ryu said. "We can't leave you by yourself."

"I will be fine." Mrs. Hamada tried to smile, but her lips trembled.

Yvonne could see the tears pooling in the corners of her eyes. "Your father wanted you to be happy in your new house. Please. Don't think of me."

That night, Yvonne slept in Ryu's childhood room. Ryu and his mother slept on futons in the room downstairs with Mr. Hamada's bones.

"You will have to learn to drive in Japan," Ryu said the next morning. "My mother has no license and if there is some emergency, then you will have to help her."

"What about you?"

"I have to work long hours. I may be too busy."

Yvonne knew that all over Japan daughters-in-law were taking care of their husbands' mothers—bathing them, preparing soft meals, doling out pills and spooning medicines into toothless mouths. The husbands were working, were drinking after hours with their co-workers in an effort to forget the heavy burdens of family and mortgage. Three generations under one roof, many hungry bellies—all this was on the husbands' shoulders. She tried to convince herself that her duty was to take care of Mrs. Hamada, but her only impulse was to run away to her new house and lock the door.

During the forty-nine days of mourning, the priest came once a week to chant for Yvonne's father-in-law. Some of the relatives came too, and everyone had to be fed. Yvonne helped in the kitchen every Sunday, dressed in black. She prepared the tray of tea and beancakes for the priest, set out slippers in a neat row in the entryway for visitors, chopped vegetables for the mourners' soup.

The fifth week, she found some carrots in the bottom of her mother-in-law's refrigerator. They'd be a good addition to the miso soup, she thought, a nice counterpart to seaweed and onions. She scrambled around in a drawer, dug up a scraper, and began peeling the carrots in long, curling strips.

Aunts and cousins bustled around her, black aprons over their mourning clothes.

"Yvonne-chan, what are you doing?" It was Kanako, there at her elbow. Her face too close to Yvonne's.

"Chopping carrots. For the soup."

"For the soup? Oh, no. There can be nothing red in the soup. Red's a color for celebration."

Yvonne stared at her for a moment. "Carrots are orange," she said.

Suzanne Kamata

"Almost red. No, no!"

The other women glanced over and nodded their agreement. Yvonne sighed. She would never understand this family or this country. She picked up a chunk of carrot, popped it into her mouth and crunched as carefully as she could. There was no way that the others could not have heard the sound, but they ignored it.

When, at last, Mr. Hamada's soul had been chanted into paradise, Yvonne waited for their lives to settle down. But things were far from normal.

"I have a duty," Ryu declared the following weekend. He was dressed in a white polo shirt and faded jeans. For once, they were wearing light-colored clothes. "I must take care of my mother. I will stay at her house three or four nights a week."

Yvonne thought that quiet and solitude would be a blessed thing. "If you must," she said. "But I will stay here."

Ryu nodded. He had given up on trying to persuade her otherwise. Or maybe he was trying to wear her down, force her to see the ridiculousness of the situation. If they lived together, she wouldn't have to learn how to drive down the right side of the road along with the maniacal motorists. She would be able to sleep next to Ryu every night. But she wouldn't budge. There was no welcome in her heart.

On Monday morning, Yvonne sat on the edge of the bed while Ryu packed. He took four pairs of balled-up socks out of the drawer and stuffed them into his duffel bag. He tossed four pairs of clean boxer shorts and his blue-striped pajamas in with the socks. She watched as he unhooked dress shirts on hangers from the closet pole. Usually, he asked her which tie went best with which shirt, but this time he chose silently.

104

Yvonne remained seated on the bed until he had departed. The house was quiet except for the sound of her breathing.

She went to work as usual, then bought a piece of chocolate cake at the bakery on her way home to eat for dinner. Why not? She deserved special treatment after seven weekends of slaving in her mother-in-law's kitchen. Back home, she lit a taper, (Ryu hated eating by candlelight, said he couldn't see the food), put on her CD of "Madame Butterfly" and arranged the wedge of cake on a china plate.

The icing was artfully arranged, but each forkful was airy and light, not the rich gooey concoction she'd hoped for. She ate slowly, scraped her plate clean of crumbs, but in the end, she wasn't quite satisfied.

There was only a plate and a fork to wash instead of the usual sinkful of dishes. There were no inside-out socks to be picked up from the floor, no rumpled newspapers to be stacked, no empty beer cans. Yvonne had all evening to do as she pleased.

After a long soak in the tub (she'd added lavender-scented salts), she sprawled across the bed with a pile of fashion magazines. She flipped through a few pages of cosmetics ads, an interview with a rising young actress that she'd never heard of, then glanced at the phone on the nightstand. It did not ring. He would not call tonight.

Ryu returned on Friday evening. As soon as she heard his car pull up next to the house, Yvonne rushed to the entryway to meet him. He pushed open the door and leaned in to kiss her. Yvonne reached for his bag.

"Mackerel," he said, sniffing the air. "We had that for dinner last night."

Yvonne bit the inside of her lips. She lugged his duffel

bag to the laundry room, but when she unzipped it, she found that all of the clothes had been freshly laundered.

"So how is your mother?" she asked when they were seated at the table.

"Sad," Ryu said. "She wants to know why you don't visit."

Yvonne's jaw tightened. "She has her precious son," she wanted to say. "What does she need me for?"

From then on the week was divided into Mrs. Hamada's days, and Yvonne's days. She knew that Japanese men, transferred by their employers to distant cities, often lived separately from their families, returning to their wives and children only on the weekends. In Japan, Yvonne and Ryu's new routine wasn't strange at all.

On Fridays, Ryu told Yvonne about taking his mother to the beauty salon, to the grocery store, to the art museum for a special exhibit of Picasso paintings.

"It's good that she's getting out and about," Yvonne said. She had stayed in the house reading books and staring out the window. Wondering if this semi-separation would go on forever.

"Yes," Ryu said. "She's smiling a bit more. She even laughed once."

"Great. Your being there must do wonders for her."

A few weeks later he started taking his mother to *ikebana* lessons. Mrs. Hamada also signed up for yoga and English conversation.

"She wants to be able to talk to you in English," Ryu said. "She's trying hard."

And then, most surprising of all, Ryu arrived home one Friday evening and announced, "My mother is going to driving school."

Driving school? At her age? She'd be embarrassed. She wouldn't last among all of those shrieking high school girls with orange-streaked hair, the boys with their pompadors and forced gruffness. Was this another ploy? Was Yvonne expected to realize that things had gone beyond all reasonable expectations, to relent, to consent to living together and driving Mrs. Hamada wherever she wanted to go?

"Tell her to do her best," Yvonne said coolly. "I'll be rooting for her."

She wondered if he was making everything up or if grief had touched him in a way that she hadn't imagined. She decided to give Mrs. Hamada a call. Just to see what was going on.

"What's this about driving school?" Yvonne asked, after enduring the niceties about health and weather.

"Oh ho ho. I'm so old. They call me granny at the school!"

"So you really are learning to drive? A car?"

"I'm trying. Maybe someday I'll be able to drive to your house."

Yvonne grimaced. "That would be great," she said. "We could speak in English."

"Oh ho ho!"

Finally, around the time when buds began to appear on the branches of cherry trees, Ryu came home on Friday night and stayed till Tuesday. On Wednesday evening, he was still at home. Yvonne had made beef stew and he'd eaten two bowls of it. Now, he was bathed, in his striped pajamas, and sitting in front of the TV with a can of beer.

Yvonne was afraid to ask when he was going back to his mother's house, but she had to know. She sat down on the sofa beside him.

"How is your mother?" she asked. At first, Yvonne thought that Ryu hadn't heard. His eyes were fixed on news footage of a war in some distant country. The sound of gun shots blasted through the room.

"Ryu?"

"My mother is fine," he said, at last. "She's decided to go on a tour to Malaysia next month with her friends." He chuckled. "She wants to go all over the world."

Mrs. Hamada? Yvonne felt something like envy rising in her gorge. Mr. Hamada's death had set her free. She was a fool to think that her mother-in-law needed Yvonne and Ryu to take care of her. Her world had suddenly burst open—a gallery of adventures waiting to be had.

Ryu's eyes were once again on the television screen. Relief workers were carrying injured Africans on stretchers while bombs exploded in the distance. After a few seconds, the carnage gave way to a shot of a suited announcer behind a desk, then a commercial featuring a muscle-bound actor exclaiming over sausages in a pan. Ryu reached for the remote control and flipped to a documentary—rare birds nesting on the Galapagos Islands, a strange and beautiful place.

Yvonne had thought that the new house was a sanctuary, but it had become like a fortress. She had imprisoned herself. She turned to Ryu, a sudden wildness in her eyes. "Give me your keys," she said.

"My keys?" He raised his eyebrows. "You're not going anywhere are you?"

She shrugged.

He hesitated for a moment before reaching into his pocket and fishing them out. He pitched them to her.

It was dark outside, the sky spangled with stars. The full

moon shone upon Yvonne. She stood still for a moment, feeling the night breeze ruffle her hair, and then moved toward the car. It sat in the driveway, big and patient, like a promise. The moon's reflection bounced off the hood. Yvonne went around to the driver's side, unlocked the door, and eased in behind the dashboard. Just sitting there with her fingers fitted into the ridges of the steering wheel made her heart pound. She could hear the blood rushing through her head. Yvonne remained seated there until the beat had slowed, then took a deep breath and went back into the house.

"What were you doing?" Ryu asked when she tossed him the keys.

"Nothing," she said. But next time, she would start the engine.

Mandala

Mandala

I came upon the Francisco de la Peña Hospital by accident, though some might say it was fate. I was riding my bicycle through back streets, on my way to the supermarket. I didn't even know at first what I had found. A block or so away from the flashing neon of the town's only pachinko parlor, and across the street from a lot full of rough marble slabs that would be used for tombstones, there was a sad-looking building set back from the road. The lot in front was overgrown with weeds.

A plane—something that might have been flown during WWII—sat in the courtyard. I got off my bike and leaned it against the stone wall, then ventured closer for a look at the plane.

I'd thought at first that the place was abandoned, though it's hard to imagine land going unclaimed and unused in a country where living space is scarce. I was standing there, staring at the plane, which turned out to be an American relic, when I heard gobbling behind me. I turned to see a turkey strutting toward me, and more turkeys farther off, hidden by the long, swaying weeds. They had a little coop, I saw, and a trough of feed.

Turkeys. How absurd. I'd thought that there was no more laughter left in me, but I laughed. I wondered who was looking after the birds.

Then I saw a man in a white coat. He had white hair, which was unusual. Most people dyed their hair black at the first sign of gray. I'd been amazed when I'd first arrived that Japanese hair stayed black for so long. I'd thought, at first, that the raven hair on my seventy-year-old neighbor was natural. I'd thought it might have had something to do with radiation; she'd survived the bombing of Nagasaki.

This man walked up to me and held out his hand. I could see myself in his glasses. My brown hair was wind-blown and wild. I wasn't wearing any make-up and I suddenly felt exposed.

"I'm Dr. Nakanishi," he said. "Welcome to my hospital."

He said it as if he were the owner of a restaurant or the docent of some museum. I guess it was a museum, in a way.

"I'm Jane Sumida," I said.

He nodded. "I know."

Our town was small and I was one of only ten foreigners living there. The others were Filipino brides, Chinese students, and a Kiwi guy who'd married a woman from Okinawa. Sometimes my picture appeared in the town's newsletter, like after I won the hundred-yard-dash in the women's twenty-thirty-year-old age group in the annual sports festival. Or after I taught a group of housewives how to prepare a Thanksgiving turkey. Not that anyone celebrated

Thanksgiving around here. Not that it was even possible to get a turkey for roasting without ordering from Kobe a month or so in advance.

You might say that I was famous there. When the divorce came through, I'd probably be notorious. I taught English to students in all three elementary schools and so just about every child in that town knew my name. They told their parents about me. The parents told their friends. It was no great surprise that Dr. Nakanishi knew who I was.

I didn't ask where the doctor had learned to speak English. His father, also a doctor, was known to be a great traveler, and I figured the son had taken after him. The father was head of some sort of English Society. He was a member of the Lions Club and Town Council. He thought up the idea of having native speakers teach the schoolchildren English. I guess I was indebted to him.

"Would you like to come inside? Have a cup of tea?"

"Sure." I had nothing better to do. I propped up my bicycle on its kickstand and followed him into the entryway of the hospital. Shoes weren't allowed inside, so I took off my sneakers, shoved them into the cubby just inside the door, and slid my feet into a pair of pink plastic slippers that were provided for guests. The doctor had his own slippers. They were tweed and looked too hot in that warm weather.

There was a car in the hospital lobby. It was an old car, a Model T, something that you might see in a small town parade back where I'd grown up in Michigan.

Dr. Nakanishi noted my interest. "Do you like it?"

"Yeah, sure," I said, wondering what it was doing in such a place.

"If you want, you can sit in it," he said.

I realized that he was offering me a privilege. The car was roped off. There was a little sign in front with a red X superimposed over a picture of a hand—"No Touching."

I didn't want to sit in the car. I would have felt ridiculous sitting in an antique Ford in a Japanese hospital on such a sweltering day. And what if I scratched it, or something? It was obviously very special to him. "No, thank you," I said. "Maybe next time."

He didn't seem to mind my refusal. He just nodded and led me into his office. I'd expected black vinyl sofas, like in the principals' offices at the schools where I worked, but the furniture here was lavender plush. A framed Andy Warhol print of Marilyn Monroe leaned against one wall, which reminded me that his father was an art collector. Maybe Dr. Nakanishi, the son, was an art lover, too. A display case hung from another wall with three shelves of tea cups in different designs. The doctor sat behind his desk. I sat on one of the purple sofas.

I wanted to ask about his patients. So far, I hadn't seen any. Maybe he wasn't a real doctor and this wasn't a real hospital. Maybe it was just a place where he kept turkeys. I looked at the walls trying to find some sort of certificate proving that he was qualified to practice medicine. All I saw were a few abstract designs framed on the wall. They were bright blue with red figures at the center. I thought they might be art. "What are those?" I asked.

Dr. Nakanishi jumped out of his chair and pointed at one of the red figures. "See this?" he said.

I nodded.

"It's a ghost."

He explained that the pictures had been taken with a special camera that recorded heat. The infra-red images were phantoms. No one had been visible when the pictures were taken.

"Huh." I glanced at the door. I was starting to get nervous.

"So what's the matter with you?" he asked, bending to look into my eyes.

It took me a moment before I realized that he thought I had come as a patient. He didn't know that I had just stumbled across the place, that I'd just stopped by for a quick look.

"Nothing," I lied.

A couple of month ago, I'd been in another hospital in another town. This place was brick, with a patch of neatly trimmed grass and well tended flowerbeds along the sidewalk leading to the front door. The doctor didn't have any cars or turkeys or pictures of Marilyn Monroe, let alone ghosts, in his hospital. He wore a white coat too, just like Dr. Nakanishi, but his hair was black, probably dyed. I'd let him come at me with needles and knives. I'd let him dig into my abdomen and take a video of my insides.

"See this here?" he'd said. "This is where your tubes are blocked off."

I didn't understand the video. I thought, "How pink!" I'd never seen my insides before, and I expected the color to be a deeper red, like blood.

"I'm sorry," the other doctor said, "but you will never be able to get pregnant I the usual way."

I spent five days in the other hospital, and when I left, I felt worse than when I'd gone in.

My husband Tamotsu took the news hard.

"We could adopt," I suggested a little too brightly, still in my hospital bed. "You can do it over the Internet these days."

I had, in fact, already scoped out websites and fallen in love with a saucer-eyed Indian orphan and a Chinese girl with only one leg.

My husband stood at the window, hands deep in his pockets. I could hear the jingle of coins against keys. He didn't say anything. I figured he was in shock like me. Overwhelmed with sadness, too choked up to speak.

"Or we could try in vitro fertilization," I said.

Finally, Tamotsu turned to me, his face so scrunched up that his eyebrows were almost touching. Like two fuzzy black caterpillars trying to kiss, I thought. "Jane," he said, "this isn't working. I want a divorce."

I realized later that there hadn't been much glue between us. Having a baby was meant to be our clichéd attempt at revitalizing our marriage. To tell the truth, our relationship had been pretty much doomed from the night we drunkenly ran into each other at a wedding party—the night we met. We'd managed to turn a mutual penchant for Toyotas and fermented soy beans (which stink to high heaven, but are actually quite tasty when mixed with raw egg and soy sauce and poured over rice) into a grand passion that had somehow led to wedlock.

Not long after my operation, Tamotsu told me about his lover. All those nights when he'd claimed to be playing mah-jongg till dawn, he'd been with the other woman. I don't think it would have bothered me so much if she'd been Japanese, but she wasn't. She was foreign, like me. A Russian with bottle blonde hair working as a hostess in one of those cramped little bars downtown. She was good at karaoke, he said. She could sing better than I could.

Back in Dr. Nakanishi's office, I finished my tea and set my cup down on the table.

"Maybe you'd like to try out Healthy Rhythm Class," he said.

"Is that your prescription for me?" I asked with a smile.

He shrugged. "Perhaps you are suffering from stress."

On the way out, another photo caught my eye. It was of a patch of land backed by craggy mountains. The color had faded a bit, as if it was old. It seemed to be of nothing in particular.

"Where's that?" I asked.

Dr. Nakanishi stood and came to my side. "Nepal," he said. "It's the future site of the Nakanishi-Nepal Friendship School. In fact, the building is probably almost finished by now."

So he was a philanthropist. And maybe a quack. In spite of myself, I was intrigued. I picked up a brochure about the Healthy Rhythm Class on my way out.

In the days to come, I asked around. "What kind of doctor is Nakanishi-sensei?"

My neighbor, the one who'd survived the atomic bomb at Nagasaki, tapped her temple.

"He's cuckoo?" I asked.

"No, it's a hospital for people who are mentally ill. Or tired."

I'd interrupted her gardening. She was crouched by the side of her house with a trowel, digging up weeds, but she put down her tool to talk to me.

She told me about the Thallosso Therapy Institute the doctor was planning on setting up by the seashore. Patients would be able to swim with dolphins and enjoy mineral baths and an herbal garden overlooking the Inland Sea. Dr. Nakanishi, it seemed, was not only full of novel ideas, but also wealthier than I'd imagined.

"By the way," my neighbor said, "Where's your husband? We haven't seen him around lately."

I wondered whom "we" referred to. She lived alone. I supposed she wasn't talking about the black rabbit that hopped around on her rice straw mats or the canary in a cage. The conspicuous absence of my husband was obviously a topic for over-the-fence gossip. I wanted to get away from all that, but I didn't know where to go. Back home in the States, I'd have to explain everything to my parents. There'd never been a divorce in my family.

"My husband is away on business," I said. A safe answer. Japanese wives often stayed behind for years when their husbands were transferred to distant prefectures.

My neighbor nodded, but I could tell that she didn't believe me.

I went to the Healthy Rhythm Class the following week, dressed in sweat pants and a headband. The other participants were already stretching in the lobby when I arrived. They were wearing pajamas. Patients, I thought. The instructor, a perky young woman with no breasts to speak of, and a high ponytail, greeted me in English. Then she giggled.

I imitated her stretches and when she pressed the button on her tape player, I tried to follow along with my body, swaying like a palm tree in a typhoon, bouncing with fake joy, bending like blades of grass under the heel of a boot.

Like me, the others exercised with what seemed to be a grim determination. No one smiled. No one, that is, except for the perky young woman.

When it was all over, I caught sight of Dr. Nakanishi. He invited me once again to join him for tea.

"So what's with the turkeys?" I asked. I was starting to

feel at home here. Comfort was making me bold.

"I thought they might make the patients happy," he said with a shrug.

"Do they?"

"I don't know. What do you think?"

Was he considering me a patient, then? I admit that the turkeys had amused me. I wondered what it would be like to live in this place, to wear those blue-striped pajamas and pink plastic slippers all day long, to linger around the vintage car in the lobby.

I decided to ask another question. "Who is Francisco de la Peña?"

"A Filipina. He saved my father's life."

It had happened during the War. Dr. Nakanishi the elder had been stationed in the Philippines as an army doctor. Because the Japanese were winning, there weren't many injured soldiers and he had a lot of free time. He treated the villagers instead. When the tables turned, the Japanese soldiers were arrested and sentenced to death. This man, Francisco de la Pena, however, argued that Dr. Nakanishi should be spared. He'd helped them, after all.

I'd never been in such a life or death situation before. I tried to imagine what it might be like to have a noose with my name on it. The details of my life, my so-called problems, suddenly seemed quite trivial.

Dr. Nakanishi the younger showed me some photos of his father and the man who'd saved him. They were young, standing with their arms draped around one another's shoulders. Tropical flowers bloomed on their shirts. The photo was old, creased, black and white and fading into gray.

I held the photo for a moment with both hands, as if it were a sacred relic, then I handed it back to him.

"Oh, and here's another picture." This time he handed me a new photo, in color, of a simple wooden building backed by mountains. Cocoa-skinned chidren, all of them barefoot, were arrayed before it. Their smiles were as dazzling as the sun overhead.

"It's the Nakanishi-Nepal Friendship School," he said proudly.

I studied those children. I wondered if they all had parents or if some of them were in need of hugs and soft words. I wondered how long it would take to get to that school from where I stood at the moment.

"Oh, by the way, some Nepalese monks are coming on Tuesday," he said. "Why don't you drop in?"

I'm not a Buddhist. I'm a lapsed Lutheran, if anything, but monks in the psychiatric hospital sounded like a spectacle.

The following Tuesday, I had a class of fifth graders. I'd planned a game of Bingo using vocabulary words dog, cat, hippopotamus, and other animal names. The game only worked if there were prizes. I usually gave out candies.

I sometimes found Japanese students to be sweetly innocent. They still liked coloring at this age, for instance, and the girls liked patty-cake games. On the other hand, they could also be stunningly rude and disrespectful, maybe because they had been brought up coddled and spoiled. Unlike the children in the Dr. Nakanishi's photo, these kids all had shoes multiple pairs of them. They took pencils and paper and native English-speaking teachers for granted.

After the Bingo game was over, the students rushed at me. "Give me candy!" they said, mobbing my desk.

"The game is over," I replied calmly. "The candy was a prize."

They ignored me and began pawing through my back-pack.

I was sure that every one of them had enough pocket money to buy an armload of candy from the store.

In the midst of all this commotion, one pig-tailed girl tapped me on the shoulder. "Teacher! Teacher!"

"Yes?" I turned to her, saw her fresh face turned up to mine like a flower to the sun.

"Do you have children?" she asked.

"No."

"Why not? Don't you and your husband have sex?"

I didn't know what to say. I had a couple more classes scheduled for that afternoon, but I couldn't take it any more. I grabbed my backpack and fought my way thorugh the jungle of limbs. Then I fled the building, hopped on my bicycle, and peddled over to the Francisco de la Pena Hospital.

The parking lot was full. Clearly, I wasn't the only one invited to behold the special guests from Nepal. I stood for a moment in the entryway, looking at all the visitors' shoes: sneakers, dull brown oxfords, shiny patent leather slings, cowboy boots. My own sandals joined them. I put on a pair of slippers and scuffed my way into the lobby.

A large circle at the center was roped off. The five monks, in their paprika and saffron robes, crouched in a ring of candles, their shaved heads bent over the work at hand. Little white bowls filled with colored sand sat at their elbows. Sticks of incense burned at intervals.

The thirty or so other spectators (some in their pajamas) and I watched in silence as they meticulously deposited colored sand with their bronze fingertips.

The mandala was half-completed. It would be a circle, I

saw, a masterpiece of temporal beauty. In the fuchsias and yellows and reds and blues I could make out flowers. The overall design was complicated, full of nesting squares and tendrils, with paisley-like flourishes.

I saw Dr. Nakanishi emerge from his office and caught his eye. He smiled and came up behind me.

"What does this mean?" I whispered.

"The gods will gather here," he whispered back, "and ease the suffering of my patients and others. Like you."

I did not necessarily believe this, but I was in awe of these men who'd come from the mountains of Nepal. I had been thinking about forever—the marriage that I thought would last that long, the children that would live beyond me and carry flowers to my grave—but this mandala would be swept away almost as soon as it was finished.

"What will happen when it's done?" I asked.

"The sand will be thrown into the river. There will be a special ceremony. Please come."

I wasn't standing on the riverbank with the others when the sand was tossed into the current. I was at home, labeling boxes and packing my belongings. I had stayed too long in this town, this country, and I was ready for a new beginning.

A few days later, I went to visit Dr. Nakanishi, to thank him and say good-bye. I wanted to express my gratitude for the stories, the green tea, and the mandala.

He didn't seem surprised to see me. As before, he asked his nurse to fetch tea, and he motioned to the purple sofa. I sat down.

I had been planning on asking about the American plane which sat in front of the hospital, but now I knew that I would not. I would make my own meaning for it. I decided that it had something to do with friendship and peace and healing. And also, flight. Travel. Movement.

"You have helped me," I said.

"Is that right?" He did not seem interested in hearing the rest. Maybe he knew all along that I would be cured by coming to this place. "I heard that you're leaving."

News travels fast in a town of this size. I nodded.

The nurse brought the tea in on a tray. She set the cups before us and then disappeared.

"Where are you going?"

I looked at the wall. The picture of the rugged mountain had been replaced by the one of the new school and its pupils. I turned back to Dr. Nakanishi. "I'll know when I get there," I said.

He nodded. "I have something for you."

I waited while he turned his back to me and rummaged in a desk drawer.

He pulled out a small plastic bag full of sand and handed it over. The colors had mixed together and blurred, no longer vivid as they had been on the floor of the hospital lobby.

"When you feel some trouble, you should release a little of this sand into the wind," he said. "It's a kind of prayer."

I studied the packet for a moment, marveling over its power, and thanked him. Then I finished my tea and we shook hands. He saw me to the entryway and watched me leave.

On the way back to my house, the place that was no longer home, I stopped by the river. I dumped the sand into my palm and rubbed it against my skin, remembering the god-invoking patterns it had made. And then I hurled it— every single grain—into the water.

For a long time, I'd imagined my heart as a red paper

Valentine torn in half. Now I realized that it was pink like the organs in the video, pumping blood through my body, and keeping me alive.

I wasn't going to be needing that sand.

You're So Lucky

You're So Lucky

Dr. Nakagawa (Dr. "In the River," you translate in your head) is the man who's supposed to keep your children alive. When you first see him, the word that pops into your head is "young." He has brush-cut hair and dimples. His ample belly strains against the pink smock. From the back, you can see that he's wearing a T-shirt underneath—casual clothes when professionalism would seem to dictate button-downs and neck-ties. Get my babies out of here, you think. You'll take them to the Citizen's Hospital on the other side of the city, to gray-templed physicians and decades of experience. But then you see that your newborn twins are trussed up with wires and tubes. There's a long thin tube going into each tiny mouth conveying oxygen to their lungs. Miniscule IV needles are threaded into their veins. There are wires linking heartbeats to monitors. Those babies aren't going anywhere. You'll have to trust this man.

Japan, the country you have lived in for ten years, has never felt so foreign as it did on the day when you were forced to check into one of its hospitals.

"Threatened premature labor," the doctor told you, and you gasped because you were only six months pregnant.

You had been planning on starting a program of Mozart and poetry in the seventh month, had already picked out a layette in the Lands' End mail order catalog. You had just started wearing maternity clothes and ordered a gray cotton dress which hadn't even arrived yet. You had an appointment the next week with a doula recommended by your hippie friend who lives in the mountains.

According to your pregnancy diary, the lungs had not yet fully developed. Your babies eyes were still closed. The ultrasound indicated that one of your unborn babies is less than a pound, the other barely over two.

Most Japanese women go back to their childhood homes to give birth. They spend the early weeks of motherhood in the rooms where they first dreamed of bouquet-bearing suitors and careers in film. Their husbands go to work and make phone calls at night.

You wanted to stay near your husband, and besides, your insurance wouldn't cover childbirth in another country. You'd picked out a small ladies' clinic locally famous for its good food (ice cream bars every afternoon, celebratory red snapper right after the baby is born). The rooms have floral curtains and you can almost pretend you're staying at a cozy B & B instead of a hospital.

You settle in with a stack of novels and silk bed jackets. Your Japanese mother-in-law shows up every day with cream puffs and freshly laundered pajamas. She sits by your bed for hours, long after you have run out of things to say to one another.

You read, you eat, you have exams. And then the doctor tells you that you must leave. The bleeding has not abated. You'd be better off in the ward of a bigger hospital—one with incubators and a Neo-Natal Intensive Care Unit.

"I like it here," you protest. "And I like you."

The doctor shakes his head. "No. You should go."

Two hospitals nearby are equipped to deal with premature babies. One is a teaching hospital boasting the latest techniques and machinery; the other is the Citizen's Hospital. While you don't relish the idea of med students traipsing in and out of your room, in the end you have no choice. There are no beds available in the maternity ward of the other hospital.

So you are transferred by ambulance, siren singing you along the highway. Because you are horizontal, you can not see the other cars making way.

Your mother has never seemed as far away as she does on the day you are rushed into the operating theater. A few weeks of bed rest have suddenly turned into blood running down your legs and an emergency Caesarean, and you are desperate for the safe and familiar.

Fortunately, your husband is only a phone call away. He arrives shortly after the obstetrician, called in a on a Saturday, still in his day-off clothes—a striped polo shirt and khakis. You see your husband long enough to tell him that you are sorry about the failure of your body to keep the babies inside. You tell him about the pain that is about to crack you apart. You press your wedding ring into his palm and then you are wheeled away.

The nurses in white run with the gurney down one corridor and the next, into a darker part of the hospital that is unfamiliar to you. There, you are handed off to another set of nurses and they take you the rest of the way.

On the operating table, you are surrounded by strangers wearing blue gauze masks and matching smocks. You look at the clock: 5:30a.m.

The nurse tells you to curl into a ball and you do and the needle slides into your spine. You wonder if you'll be able to speak Japanese under anesthesia.

You'd expected childbirth to be something else entirely— Enya on the stereo, champagne chilling in the hospital mini-fridge, your husband's fingers kneading the small of your back. Instead, he is in another room and the obstetrician is swabbing and slicing your abdomen. There is a screen between you and the action so you can't see a thing. You feel liquid ooze and gush, and the hands of the doctor reaching into your womb. There is movement, like a fish flopping against your belly, and then a tiny mewling cry.

"*Kawaii*," the doctor says. "Cute." But you can only imagine because your son is immediately whisked off to an incubator before you can catch a glimpse of him.

"Now we're going in for the other one," the doctor says, and he reaches for the girl who has lived beneath your heart for the past few months. And then she is taken away, too, and the worst part is over. Or so you think.

Your mother-in-law arrives for her daily visit before your husband has a chance to call her with the news. You hear the rustle of plastic bags filled with oranges and yogurt and then you hear her gasp. When you open your eyes, you see that she is looking at you as if you are dying.

You have never been so thirsty in your life, but the nurses say "No drinking or eating." Your legs are still numb from the anesthesia. When your mother-in-law pours you a cup of juice and urges you to drink, you have to remind yourself that it's a gesture of kindness, not torture.

Over the next few days and weeks you will spend more time with your mother-in-law than anyone else.

The first time you see your babies, see the swell of their eyeballs under sealed eyelids, you think "baby bird." And then you look at their thin, bowed legs and think "bull frog." Their heads, so narrow, so large in proportion to their bodies: aliens.

They have little beards, but no eyelashes. When your daughter's diaper is changed, you see that she has no labia. You can't make out the shape of their mouths which are taped to the breathing tubes.

Your husband was right. They do not look like the babies on the covers of your magazines, but you are wrenched with a violent kind of love. If you could will them back into your body, you would. You are sorry you dreaded the pain of child-birth. Let them tear you apart if they could be born again, healthy.

The Neo-Natal Intensive Care Unit nurses' photos are tacked to the wall. In several of the snapshots, the nurses are holding the pale-skinned black-haired baby next to your son's incubator. He is a giant—six or seven pounds at least. Your son weighs less than two pounds.

The nurse in charge of your boy is Ms. Matsumoto. She goes about her work with the enthusiasm of a kindergarten teacher. She dances with the giant baby to the tune of "Braham's Lullaby" and takes him for "walks." She reaches into your son's incubator and waves his hand around as if he were an action figure. "*Genki da yo!*" she says in a baby boy's voice. "Don't worry! I'm fine!"

Sometimes Nurse Matsumoto teases Dr. Nakagawa. This seems bizarre in a country where authority demands respect. You wonder if they are flirting, even though there is no word for "flirt" in the Japanese language. Most of the NICU staff is young and you wonder if they have affairs with each other like the nurses and doctors in the TV show "ER." You wonder if they are married. No rings are allowed in the NICU so it's difficult to tell. No watches, either. Everyone must wear a pink smock over their clothes (pink being a color found to be soothing to babies), a white cap over their hair. The parents wear masks. You have to wash your hands three times before you can touch your babies.

Every three hours, you and the other new mothers go to The Nipple Room. Okay, so it's not really called that; it has some Japanese name that you can never remember, but the Nipple Room seems apt.

All five or six of you (the number varies) sit on cushioned benches with your pajamas unbuttoned and your pink/brown nipples bared. There is none of the modesty that you've experienced in women's locker rooms in Japan. You compare and admire each others' breasts.

"Mine are so hard," one woman moans. "Feel them."

At her urging, you press the pads of your fingers against her swollen breast and indeed, it is solid.

When the nurse hands over her giant baby boy, she tickles his parted lips with her nipple, but he won't suck.

"Don't sleep," she says. "Give me some relief."

You are jealous that she has a baby to suckle even if he is reluctant. You sit there beside her eking colostrum from your own breasts. It slides into the sterilized bottle, thick and yellow, drop by precious drop. Your fingers ache. Your lily white breasts are stained with bruises.

You've heard that thoughts of babies activate the ducts, make the milk flow faster, so you think about your son and daughter.

Your boy has a slender tube through his nose which goes directly to his stomach. Every two hours, he is fed two milliliters of your milk. Two cubic centimeters—that's maybe a teardrop or as much dew as falls on one leaf of clover.

This morning when you sat before your daughter's incubator listening to the hum of the respirator, Dr. Nakagawa told you that she could not digest the milk. Although she, too, was fed through a tube from nose to stomach, the colostrum remains in her stomach, unprocessed. The feeding will be stopped. If she can't eat, how will she stay alive?

"I've heard that physical contact can make all the difference with preemies," your college roommate e-mails from New York.

You've heard that too, but you're afraid to touch your babies. You open the Plexiglas doors to your daughter's incubator and stroke her foot with one finger. She jerks away.

"I'm your mother," you whisper sadly. "I'm giving you affection."

Her eyes are still sealed shut. She can not look at you.

You caress her arms, ever so lightly, and then her head, and then brush your finger tips over her torso. The monitor alarm goes off. You look up quickly and then snatch your hand away when you see that her heart rate has suddenly dropped from 112 beats per minute to sixty.

A nurse comes running toward you, rubber soles

squeaking on the floor, and then Dr. Nakagawa.

"You'd better let her rest for awhile," he says. Then he smiles sadly, as if to assure you that it wasn't entirely your fault.

Your mother-in-law arrives with bags of souvenirs. She has spent the previous evening preparing packages of little bean-filled cakes, oranges, and iron-supplemented soft drinks for the visitors sure to stream into your room.

"It's the seventh day," she says knowingly. "And an auspicious day on the calendar."

There is still so much that you don't know about local tradition, but you are quite sure that no well-wishers will arrive. Later, you will learn that the people in the office where you worked are wondering if your babies are even alive.

It is hard to decide if this is a celebratory occasion or not.

Your parents send a bouquet of flowers and a card saying "Thank you for our new grandchildren."

You aunt calls from Michigan and her first words are "I'm so sorry."

Your mother-in-law, who has not yet seen the babies, knows only that you have provided an heir. She sits by your bed all day and puts on her social smile every time the door opens, but it is only the cleaning lady come to scrub the toilet, the handsome young intern to change your IV fluid, the nurse to take your temperature, a mischievous child who barged into the wrong room.

When your husband arrives that evening to spell her, your mother-in-law's face is heavy and sad. All of the bags that she has brought remain in a corner of the room.

A couple of days later—an unlucky day according to your mother-in-law's calendar—your hippie friend comes to visit.

The nurse, with her finger to your pulse, studies him out of the corner of her eye. What must she think of this pony-tailed man in a poet's blouse? Does she think that this is an assignation, a tryst? He has arrived with a tattered paperback of Anne Waldman under one arm and a bowl of salad in the other.

The nurse finishes her business and leaves and you lay against the white sheets while he feeds you freshly picked parsley, spinach and sprouts on a fork.

You tell him about the treatment that your children are getting.

Your hippie friend who self-medicates with herbal teas says "All those chemicals can't be good for them."

But you know that without them, your babies would die.

There is one other woman who expresses milk by hand. Her newborn son (1318 grams and growing) is in the NICU, too. His incubator is next to your baby girl's.

One day you start talking about mothers-in-law.

"My mother-in-law," you say, "sits by my bed all day. I just want to read my book, but I feel as if I should entertain her."

"My mother-in-law," you say, "is always hovering and fussing. If I so much as cough, she jumps up to throw a blanket over me even though I'm sweating. It drives me nuts."

"Mine never visits," the other woman says.

"Why not?"

"Because she blames me for this." And you know that she is referring to her own bum womb and the tiny boy behind Plexiglas.

On another day, you hear a nurse tell a story of a woman who was divorced for giving birth to a stillborn child. The husband and mother-in-law discussed it while the wife was still convalescing, still grappling with her grief, no doubt. They gave her the news the day after she was released from the hospital.

You realize that the woman who annoys you so much is not so bad after all.

You walk into the NICU in your mask and smock and paper hat and the young doctor motions you to his desk.

"Your son in fine," he says. "No problem."

And then he takes out a photo done by ultrasound, shows you the blue spots that indicate blood in your daughter's lungs. He draws a picture of the heart's chambers and scratches a word above it: "ductus arteriosis." It seems that a duct in your daughter's heart has failed to close as it should have after birth. Her body has not adapted to life outside the womb; her lungs don't understand that they must now fill with oxygen.

The doctor tells you that there is medication and, if that doesn't work, they can try surgery. He gives you a form to sign your consent.

You sit by her incubator longer than usual.

"My little sweet pea," you say. "My darling girl."

She weighs no more than a small animal—a squirrel, perhaps, or a chipmunk. You cannot imagine such a delicate being surviving cuts and sutures.

When you go back to your room, your mother-in-law is there, plumping pillows and changing the water in the vases of flowers—flowers for "congratulations" and "get well soon."

You try to smile, but your spirits are flagging. You show her the form explaining the problem and the procedure for dealing with your baby girl's heart. It is all in Japanese. You explain as well as you can that there is a duct that needs to be closed. You try to be brave and confident because you know how much your mother-in-law will worry if you aren't.

The next day when you visit your children, Dr. Nakagawa is listening to opera in his office. You can hear Italians warbling through the partition and you try to identify the music. A tragedy? A comedy? Is this one of those stories where the heroine dies consumptive at the end?

The other four babies in the NICU have been released from their Plexiglas prisons. They are given suck at intervals by cheerful moms, taken on promenades by the nurses, bathed in the stainless steel sink. If Dr. Nakagawa is worried, it's because of your children. It's because of the baby girl balanced between heaven and life on earth.

But then the young doctor emerges from his haven and smiles.

"Your son," he says, "no problem."

"And my daughter?"

"Getting better."

Yesterday's tears were tears of fear and sorrow and worry, but today's are something else altogether.

On the fourth day, the ultrasound reveals that the duct has closed completely. The treatment was a success.

You are exhausted from midnight and three and six a.m. milkings, from the heart-pumping drama you've been forced to endure, from the bedside hovering of your mother-in-law. When you find her, once again plumping pillows, changing water, rearranging toiletries and so on, you explain in your best Japanese that the duct in your daughter's heart has closed. And then you tell her that you want to take a nap. She nods gravely and leaves you alone in the shuttered room.

You sleep. When your mother-in-law returns an hour later, you see that she has been crying. She tells you that she has been wandering the hospital halls worrying about your baby girl.

"The duct closed," you say. "It's a *good* thing."

So now your daughter is getting better. She is being fed breast milk. She is growing stronger.

But then the doctor tells you that although the duct in your son's heart closed on its own, it has now reopened.

"That can happen?" you ask.

"Yes, sometimes. But rarely."

You feel helpless, much like you do when an earthquake rocks your house. Everything is unpredictable, subject to chance.

You are given another form to sign. On this day you sit next to your son's incubator longer than usual.

On the day that you come home from the hospital, your next-door neighbor is weeding her flower bed. She sees you get out of the car with your little brown suitcase. She looks from your face to your diminished stomach, wipes her hands on her pants, and ambles over.

"Congratulations," she says. "A boy and a girl at once. You're so lucky."

Your neighbor had a baby just this side of forty after years of trying. She has a five-year-old girl and from what she's implied, there'll be no more children. There is an aura of envy around her.

"They're still in the hospital," you say. "They're on life support."

She waves away your concern. "They'll be fine. These days incubators are just like the mother's womb."

You reflect upon this. Inside, the body is warm and dark.

The incubator is in brightly lit space. Sometimes the nurses wrap gauze around your babies' feet and hands because their extremities chill easily. Inside the body, babies are lulled by the mother's heartbeat and the sound of her voice. The NICU is a cacaphony of alarms and beeps and buzzes and infants screaming in pain.

After you leave the hospital, everyone you run into asks "Why?" Why did you go into premature labor? Why were your babies born fourteen weeks early?

Your older woman friend thinks it's because you let your legs get cold. She saw you at a musical in February in a knee-length dress and nothing but nylons when you should have been wearing insulated pants.

Your boss believes it's because you walked to work each day—a five minute saunter, if that—carrying a soft-sided briefcase containing notebooks and a magazine or two. He doesn't consider that the cigarette smoke perpetually fogging the office might have had something to do with it. You have a flashback of a cup of coffee downed at your desk in the third month and you wonder if that might be it.

Your husband thinks it's because you went to an African dance party the week before you started to bleed. You knew when you walked to the bus stop and later when you boarded the train, that your husband wouldn't approve. But he was in Hokkaido on business, and you would have been alone. Better to be among caring friends, you'd thought.

Maybe you shouldn't have moved the furniture when your husband called and said, "The new recliner will be delivered in ten minutes. Clear out a space."

But then you think about your sister-in-law who traveled to Bolivia on business in her seventh month of pregnancy, who rested her wine glass on the shelf of her stomach in between sips of Chardonnay, who actually went jogging till a few days before giving birth. Her son, your nephew, was born after two hours of labor.

Who is the freak of nature? You or your sister-in-law? And how can something so ordinary, so natural, go so wrong?

The giant baby is transferred from the NICU to the floor above, to pediatrics. On the day of his departure, you watch his mother dress him in striped blue pajamas. She packs up his stuffed bear and the mobile that played Braham's lullaby loud enough for the other babies to hear, and then they are gone.

In a few days the doctor will try to take the tube out of your daughter's lungs.

Without the tube, you can see that your daughter's mouth is shaped like Clara Bow's. It's a beautiful mouth. Until now, she has sucked on the tube for solace, but now she gapes like a fish out of water.

"Her mouth is lonely," the nurse says.

You wish you could slide your pinky between her lips.

For the first few hours, she takes regular breaths on her own. But in the days that follow, she sometimes forgets to inhale. When she stops breathing, the monitor beeps. You step aside quickly to allow the nurse to reach in and jiggle her. After a moment, her chest rises and falls, and you start breathing again, too. It takes awhile to get used to it, but you do. Soon, you are the one to reach in and remind her to breathe.

You are singing to your daughter, making up the words as you go along: "My darling child, my little peanut, my ballerina girl."

Suddenly, the doors whoosh open. In comes the young doctor, a flock of nurses and a pair of incubators. Another set of twins has been born, alas, too early. You stop singing and sit frozen like a bird in the bush.

The doctor calls out for things and the nurses hand them over. Each baby is weighed. With-in five minutes, both red-skinned newborns are intubated and set up with IVs. You admire the staff's brisk competence. This must be what it was like on the day of your babies' birth.

The new twins, you notice, two boys, are slightly larger than your son was at birth. Your daughter remains the smallest patient in the NICU. You want to seek out the parents and tell them that you know how they feel.

"But look!" you'd say. "Our boy was smaller still and now he thrives!"

His mouth twitches in a smile. His hand curls around your finger.

The mother is wheeled in on a gurney, up close to the incubators. You watch her reach inside to touch each one and think, "How lucky! I had to wait till I was able to walk by myself to see my children."

But then the heart specialist is called in. He and the other doctors confer behind screens. They speak in hushed tones to the twins' parents.

When you visit two days later, one of the new twins is missing. In its place is an incubator covered with vinyl.

You know that it is none of your business, but you gesture and ask, "What happened to the other one?"

The nurse frowns at you with your bad manners. She makes a stalling sound—"mmmm"—and you lower your eyes.

"Oh," you say. "Pardon me."

In that same week, another baby dies and your daughter's kidneys stop functioning.

Your daughter's face is puffy with water; her diapers remain dry. Two days ago she was delicate and slender. Now, the nurses joke that she looks like a sumo wrestler.

"We've never seen anything like this before," Dr. Nakagawa tells you. "In most cases, kidney failure occurs immediately after birth, not two months later."

"What's causing it?" you ask.

He answers with the most chilling words yet: "We don't know."

This is a country where doctors pretend to be gods, a condition which makes his frankness all the more alarming. For once in your life, you would have preferred a lie, some fake confidence.

When milk time comes around, your daughter gets nothing. She is being fed intravenously until her condition improves.

The doctor tells you that your son is almost ready to go home. You have nearly forgotten that these days will end, that you are the true guardian of the baby boy and girl in the incubators. The thought of taking care of them by yourself—the responsibility—terrifies you.

You are sitting, watching your daughter's miniature chest rise and fall, when you see something black out of the corner of your eye. It's a fly. You think, at first, that it's in the incubator with your baby, but then you notice that it's crawling up the blinds.

"Hey!" you call out, in a panic. "There's a fly in here!"

Flies carry germs. Flies cause African Sleeping Sickness

and other diseases that could kill your children.

One of the nurses, the one who is always impeccabl made-up, strolls over. "Where?" she asks. Her voice is calm.

You point to the winged vermin now exploring the top of your daughter's incubator.

The nurse takes a rolled up notebook and swats. The fly is dead. You breathe a sigh of relief.

"How'd it get in here?" you ask. The windows are sealed.

"It must have followed one of you mothers in here," she says. "Maybe it likes the smell of your milk."

A couple days later, when you go to another part of the hospital for insurance purposes, you see a kitten in the corridor. A kitten: Fleas, mites, toxoplasmosis.

"Nurse," you call out to a young woman in starched white. "There's a cat in here!"

The nurse looks in the direction you are waving in.

"So there is," she says with a smile. "How cute!" And then, believe it or not, she walks away, off to the ladies' room.

You wonder if you are being paranoid. You wonder if you will be able to protect your son—and later your daughter—from all the black flies and kittens and other dangers in the world.

Your son begins breathing room air, unassisted. He is taken out of the incubator and installed in a Plexiglas bed. He starts drinking breast milk from a bottle and then, little by little, from your breast. He cries loudly whenever he is hungry and you worry that he might be disturbing the other babies who are weaker and sicker.

Dr. Nakagawa tells you that when your baby boy reaches 2,500 grams, he can go home. He now tips the scale at 2,300.

You haven't finished preparing the nursery yet, but this

news brings a bloom to your cheeks. It's been almost three months since he departed your body and you long to have him close again.

Dr. Nakagawa asks you if you'd like to schedule his release for an auspicious day on the Japanese calendar. You are not superstitious like your mother-in-law, but you know that she would be horrified if your son left the NICU on an unlucky day. You are not superstitious, but you are willing to take all the help you can get.

The medicine that the doctors prescribed for your daughter has worked. Her kidneys are functioning properly once again and her second chin has melted. Her milk intake is increased. She is getting better, but you take nothing for granted. There have been too many surprises along the way. Every day your husband chants Buddhist sutras and you pray to another deity while on your knees.

A couple weeks later, your daughter begins to acquire the suggestion of meat around her thighs. At last, she develops labia and grows eyelashes.

By the day that your son is ready to check out of the hospital, your tiny baby girl is out of the incubator as well, engulfed in a gauze kimono and swaddled in a white bath towel.

You dress your son in baby clothes for the first time. The little sailor outfit is intended for a preemie, but it is roomy on your boy.

You and your husband give the NICU staff a box of cream puffs and a case of soft drinks as an infinitesimal token of your appreciation. Insurance has pretty much picked up the tab for your children's care, but you want to pay back something.

Everyone gathers round as you prepare to take your boy out. You can't speak because your throat is jammed shut by emotion. Instead, you bow and let the doctors and nurses see the tears in your eyes.

You hold your daughter a little longer than usual on this day. She looks up at you with clear gray eyes. You wonder if she will notice that her brother, her wombmate, is no longer in the next bed, and if she will cry out in the night. Twins belong together, you think, but for now, they must separate. When she has closed her eyes and drifted into sleep, you force yourself to put her down until tomorrow morning.

You tuck your son into a wicker basket with a comforter printed with a teddy bear motif. Then you carry him out the whooshing door. When you step onto the elevator with your baby-boy-in-a-basket, it feels like you are doing something illegal.

You can now hold, feed, and bathe your son whenever you want to. The nurses no longer have any say. Dr. Nakagawa's work is done. Now it's up to you to keep him alive.

Outside, cars and trucks drive past. The grass is green. Swallows swoop overhead and the sound of giggles floats over from a nearby kindergarten. It's late summer and the sun is shining on your child for the first time.

The Naming

The Naming

When Coach Hideki Yamada arrived at his office at Kita High School, a rosy glow was just blooming on the horizon. He'd slept only a few hours the night before, having stayed at the hospital with Christine until midnight, after which he'd gone home and worried over his batting order for another couple of hours. But now, he'd downed a can of hot coffee and the caffeine mixed with adrenaline was shooting through his veins. He was ready. In spite of the team's 0-19 win-loss history, he couldn't wait to gather up his players, all twelve of them, and get on that bus to Awaji Island.

He'd booked a game with a school coached by one of his college teammates. They hadn't seen each other in years. He was looking forward to seeing his friend and rehashing those glory days, even if his players were sure to lose.

Through the window he could see some of his guys rolling in on their one-speed bicycles, their figures murky in the dawn. He felt a stab of tenderness for them. These were the boys who'd stuck by him week after week, month after month, while they lost to larger, more experienced teams. The diehards, who'd outlasted the fifteen or twenty kids who'd almost immediately dropped out. The pioneers. Maybe their dads had told them how Coach Yamada had once been an ace pitcher himself. He'd been locally famous in high school, and then he'd gone on to Tsukuba University where he'd been named to the All-Star team. Coach Yamada knows baseball, they might tell their sons. Just give him a chance.

Before he'd been hired at this brand new high school to put together a team from scratch, first year students only, Hideki had coached weight lifting. Although he'd become a high school teacher with the express goal of becoming a baseball coach, there weren't any openings when he was first employed. He'd been disappointed initially. Weight lifting was a minor sport; winning a meet didn't bring the same kind of glory as a soccer or a baseball victory. You'd never see the All-Shikoku weightlifting tournament on TV, whereas it seemed every television and radio in the nation was tuned in to the national high school baseball tournament at Koshien. Even so, he'd grown to love his job.

One day, this burly kid ambled into his weight room asking to join the team, and after a couple of years, Yamada had turned him into a national champion. They'd gotten newsprint. The kid had gone on to compete in China. He'd been awarded a full scholarship to college.

Coaching weight-lifting had turned out to be immensely satisfying, so that when he'd been offered this new position—first ever baseball coach at a newly opened high school—he'd hesitated at first. But he took the job. So now here he was, fumbling along, full of doubts. He no longer went to the movies with his wife, no longer had time for weekend junkets with her to nearby islands. He devoted himself to this fledgling team, while the parents complained his practice sessions were cutting into study time.

Even his wife grumbled.

"Why does baseball have to be so time-consuming?" Christine had asked several months earlier as he dragged in after dark. "In the United States, it's a summer sport, so why does it have to take up the whole year here?"

She'd left his supper on the table, covered in plastic wrap. Her own dirty dishes were in the sink.

"Your practice sessions and weekend games don't leave any time for family."

"My team is my family," he'd blurted.

She'd turned away, seeming to wilt a little, and he realized how much his words had wounded her. By then they'd been trying for over two years to conceive.

He'd sat down at the table and peeled back the plastic to reveal cold gray meat edged by congealed fat. Normally, she would have warmed it up for him, but he decided to eat it cold as a kind of penance for what he'd said.

"I meant my *second* family," he amended, but it was too late.

Most of these kids were college-bound. Frankly, most of them had no talent. Once in a while he felt almost contemptuous of their clumsiness, their lack of motivation. When he'd played ball, the coach had practically dragged him off the field each day at the end of practice. He was always the last to leave. These kids were different. They didn't love the game the way he did. The ones who lived for baseball went to Seiko High School or Naruto Tech.

"You should try to make it more fun," Christine said. "It's a game, for crying out loud. I've seen those baseball players at the high school where I teach running around with tires hitched to their shoulders. They look like prisoners in a gulag."

"You don't understand," he'd told her. He remembered how he'd hated dragging those tires around himself, and yet what remained most vivid in his memory was a sense of brotherhood, of accomplishment. He and his teammates had been as self-disciplined as monks.

Now he pulled his uniform out of his duffel bag. He'd been doing his own laundry these days, ever since his wife had gone into the hospital. He'd been washing her clothes, too—her underwear and pajamas; she didn't like wearing the hospital garb. As he turned on the washing machine, he remembered how his mother used to bend over the sink in the evenings, rubbing hard at the dirt smudging the knees of his uniform. She never complained, even though the bleach made her skin flaky and dry.

He stripped off his sweatshirt and changed into his uniform.

Outside, the rented bus rumbled into the parking lot. He went out to meet the driver. Miki, his assistant coach, was just getting out of his car. Hideki and Miki had played on the same team in high school. After graduating, Miki had taken over his father's trucking business, but he helped out with a local Little League team in his free time. Hideki hadn't talked to him all that much in the intervening years, but when Miki had volunteered his services, he'd had been happy to take him up on it.

"How's your wife?" he asked.

"She says bed rest is boring, but she's doing okay," Hideki replied. "And yours?"

Miki grimaced. He was leaving his harried wife home with three little kids, including a baby. Since he was his own boss, he made his own hours, but he didn't devote a lot of time to his young family. According to Miki, his wife was always ranting.

"You'll see." Miki chucked his shoulder.

Hideki allowed himself a momentary vision of Christine with their twins. He pictured a little girl, demure in a pinafore, and a boy the spitting image of himself at four or five, a boy in a baseball cap bouncing with energy.

"I guess it's time to round up the guys," Miki said.

Hideki nodded. The phone in his pocket began to ring. He pulled it out and flipped it open. It was from the hospital, probably his wife.

"*Hai?*"

But it wasn't Christine. A nurse was on the line.

"Your wife is about to go into surgery for an emergency C-section," she said. "You'd better come quick."

A C-section? He stood there holding the phone, uncomprehending. It was way too early, only 26 weeks into the pregnancy. He watched, unable to move, as his players filed out of the clubhouse and onto the bus.

He thought about calling his mother and asking her to go to the hospital in his place. Men of his father's generation didn't take off from work for the births of their children. Women had their babies with their mothers urging them on. But Christine would never forgive him if he didn't show up.

"I'm on my way."

"What is it?" Miki asked, glancing at the phone in his hand.

"She's having the babies now. I gotta go. Do you mind?"

Miki nudged him toward his car. "Of course not. I'll handle it."

Hideki grabbed his clothes, figuring he'd change at the hospital, then got into his car and pealed out of the parking lot. He raced all the way to the hospital, his heart hammering.

She was lying on a gurney when he arrived in the ward. The obstetrician, called in on a Saturday, greeted him in a pink polo shirt.

"She's gone into premature labor," he said in a matter-of-fact tone. "At twenty-six weeks, it'll be a challenge, but we'll do what we can to save the babies."

So blithe, Hideki thought. *As if it were just a job.* For a split second, he wanted to punch the doctor, to make him feel the same kind of ache that was spreading in his chest.

The nurse handed him a plastic bag containing Christine's wedding ring.

"No jewelry allowed in surgery," she said.

Hideki shoved it into his pants pocket and went over to his wife.

"I'm sorry," she said. "I tried…"

He shook his head, trying to smile.

"Don't worry. Everything will be all right."

And then they were rushing down the hall and around the corner to the operating room.

"You can't go in," the nurse told him. "There's a waiting room over there."

He saw the fear in Christine's eyes, saw her biting her lower lip so as not to cry. "I'll see you later," he said. Then he waved—a small, futile gesture—and sat down to wait.

He tried not to think about the scalpel slitting his wife open, the blood, the tiny bodies being extracted and lifted into the light. Instead, he held an image of her face in his mind—her face on the morning she'd come to him after taking the home pregnancy test.

"It's blue! It's blue!"

He'd hugged her and swung her around the room until he realized that maybe he should be a little gentler, considering her condition.

He had listened to her retch for weeks afterward, had watched her face go gaunt and elegant. They'd go out for spaghetti at La Pomodoro, or burgers at McDonald's, and then she'd come home and rush to the toilet. They'd known from the first ultrasound that they were expecting twins. The doctor had warned that the extra hormones would exacerbate the nausea; he hadn't been kidding.

Hideki had gone to the corner convenience store in the middle of the night to buy fruit-flavored milk, pork-filled buns, bananas—whatever she thought she might be able to keep down. On every errand he'd been filled with affection— for his wife, for his two unborn children.

Now he reached into his pocket, fingers grazing the muted cell phone, and grabbed Christine's wedding ring. He rolled it around in his hand, remembering the day when she'd told him that she was pregnant with a boy. He'd missed out on the ultrasound that day because of baseball practice.

"A boy and a girl," she'd said.

"We hit the jackpot!"

And Hideki had allowed himself to imagine playing catch in the backyard with his son. He'd even gone out and bought a child-sized mitt.

He put the ring back into his pocket and propped his elbows on his knees. He really wanted a cigarette. He'd promised Christine that he'd quit for the sake of the children, but...

Not too long ago he'd seen a documentary about preemies on TV, and so he knew that at 26 weeks, their lungs and hearts hadn't fully developed. Their eyes would still be fused shut. They wouldn't have any body fat at this stage. At 26 weeks, they'd be in all kinds of danger.

He glanced at the operating room door. There was no sign of movement. He thought briefly of going into the stairwell to call Miki and find out how the game was going, then decided against it. Miki would want to know what was happening at the hospital. Then he thought of all the other people he would have to call when this was over with—his mother, his sister, his closest friends. He'd call Shimizu first. He'd be sympathetic, at least; his wife had miscarried twice before finally delivering a healthy baby girl. And he'd call Toda, who was now a teacher at the school for the handicapped, spending his days with those twisted, drooling kids, many of whom had been born too early. He sighed, hoisted himself up and went to buy a pack of Marlboros.

Hideki was outside on a bench, lighting up his second cigarette when the call came from the NICU.

"Your babies are stabilized," a nurse told him. "You can come and see them now".

He took a drag, then put out the cigarette with the heel of his shoe and went up to the fourth floor. A nurse with bobbed hair and glasses—Nurse Matsumoto, according to her name tag—came out to guide him through the rituals of hand-washing and disinfecting. She opened a locker to reveal sterile gauze robes and slippers, and handed him a mask and a cap.

The NICU was all bright light and beeping monitors. A nurse, visibly pregnant under her pink smock, paced with a baby that was hooked up to an IV pole.

Nurse Matsumoto led Hideki to the back of the unit.

"Here they are," she said, gesturing to the two incubators in the corner.

Hideki looked up at the nurse. She was smiling, as if there was something to be happy about.

"Yamada Baby 1" was taped to the boy's incubator. On the girl's: "Yamada Baby 2."

Let them die, he thought as he peered into the Plexiglas isolettes, saw all of those wires and tubes threading into their scrawny raw bodies. Their eyes were fused shut. Their tiny heads were oddly shaped—narrow, not round. Their froggy limbs were covered with black hair. They didn't even look human. *Let them die.* They were too small; it was way too early for this. The doctor had filled him in on everything that might go wrong: bleeding in the brains, holes in the hearts, blindness, mental retardation. That is, if they made it through the night. Let them die. They'd try again. She'd gotten pregnant in the first round of in vitro fertilization. There was no reason why they couldn't succeed again. They were both healthy, more or less, only in their thirties. They had money in the bank. And if it didn't work out, he might even consider adopting. It wouldn't be the same as having a child of his own flesh and blood, and he could just imagine how his mother would feel about it, but he would do it if it would make Christine happy, if it would make up for all of this. Hadn't she tried to talk him into adopting before, when she'd first found out she couldn't conceive?

"It's the ethical thing to do," she'd said, citing third world poverty and the fuzzy morality of lab-produced embryos. She started a clip file—articles about infanticide and baby hatches in Eastern Europe for abandoned Romany infants. He'd come across her, late at night, surfing international adoption sites on the Internet.

"Sarita," she'd read aloud to him. "'She has a sunny disposition and is very clever.' We could raise an Indian girl, couldn't we? Even if she has a club foot?"

He'd shrugged, at a loss about what to do to get her mind off the foreign babies. What could she be thinking, wanting to raise a child that didn't look even remotely Japanese?

"Let's try the IVF thing. Just once. Please."

One of the babies' monitors started to beep. Hideki started at the sound, but Nurse Matsumoto opened the door to the isolette, calmly jiggled a wire, and stepped back.

"Have you decided on names yet?" she asked.

"Uh, no. Not yet."

They'd talked about names of course, he and Christine. It'd been almost a game. They'd come up with new names every week. Christine had lobbied for Amelia or Annetta, her great-grandmothers' names for the girl, but Hideki wanted to name her after a flower. Yuri, for lily. Or Sumire (violet). For the boy, Christine had suggested Jack or Nick, strong names for a strapping boy, she'd said. But Nick in Japanese would sound like the word for meat. He'd be teased endlessly.

Hideki preferred Tsuyoshi, using the Chinese characters for enduring strength.

"No one in my family will be able to pronounce that," Christine had objected.

His mother had advised them to go to a fortune teller. If they chose the wrong kanji, the effect could be disastrous, she'd said. She also told them that they'd be in trouble for hanging their laundry facing north, the land of the dead.

She hadn't gone to a fortune teller. Hideki's grandfather

had chosen his and his sister's names. That's the way it was done. But his father was dead, and his mother would never presume to take on the duties of the patriarch. Hideki was the head of the family now, the one she deferred to. The fortune teller was just a suggestion.

He'd never bring it up to Christine, though. Just the thought of her sputtering in indignation about his mother's presumption, her superstitious mind, kept him from mentioning it. He remembered how incensed she'd been about the five-month belly banding ceremony his mother had proposed.

"It sounds like Chinese foot-binding," she'd wailed. "How barbaric!"

Now, in the NICU, he ran his fingers over the label on his son's incubator and lightly rapped his knuckles on the hard plastic.

Nurse Matsumoto suddenly appeared with a Polaroid camera.

"How about a photo? For your wife?"

He shook his head, and put a hand up as if to cover the lens.

"No!" Then he reeled away and moved to the door.

The nurses exchanged glances. *This one wasn't taking it too well.*

"*Shikata ga nai*," the doctor had said. "These things happen."

Sometimes babies were born too early. Sometimes they didn't make it past the first few hours.

Christine was wan and pale against the pillows. She tried to work up a smile.

"How are they? The nurses won't let me go see them till

I can walk on my own."

Hideki detected a touch of relief in her tone. Maybe she didn't really want to see them. Maybe she was as scared as he was.

"They're fighting," he said, thinking of those tiny hands grasping at air. "They're...cute."

"Really?"

"Yeah. I mean, they don't look like those babies." He gestured to the stack of child-rearing books at her bedside, the plump infants on the covers.

She nodded.

"So what do you think about Emma?"

"Emma?"

"As a name for our daughter. After Queen Emma of Hawaii."

They'd visited the queen's summer palace on their honeymoon, and Christine, he remembered, had been captivated by her biography. She was both Anglo and Hawaiian—a multicultural woman who did good deeds.

"Sure." Hideki shrugged. What did it matter anymore? They would probably be dead by morning.

"And I've decided that I like Tsuyoshi after all."

He went closer to the bed, thinking to embrace her, to comfort her, and she scrunched up her nose.

"You've been smoking," she said. "You promised."

He sighed.

"I'm sorry. It's been quite a day."

He stayed with her for a few hours, till feeling started to return to her legs, till she urged him toward the door.

"Go get something to eat. You must be starving."

Gratefully, he made his exit. He went across the street to a little curry shop favored by interns and nurses.

After he'd placed his order, he drew out his cell phone and checked his messages. Miki had called three times. He dialed.

"So how's your wife?"

"She's doing okay," Hideki replied. "The babies are in the NICU. I'll tell you about it later. How'd the game go?"

Something rustled on the other end of the line. Papers. Game stats, maybe.

"We won."

"What?"

"Yeah, it was sweet. Ten to zero. You know how Abe's fork-ball is always a little screwy? Well, today he nailed it. Seven strike outs."

As Miki went through the game play by play, telling of Inoue's stolen base in the second inning, Tanaka's double with a runner on third, and the home run that had sent the whole team swarming in joyful disbelief, Hideki felt something swoop and soar inside of him. He choked back his emotions.

"That's great. Thank you for being there."

"No problem, man. Glad I could help."

When the food arrived, he ate quickly even though the spices singed his tongue. He had to get back over there, to the hospital. He wanted to tell Christine that something good had happened today.

His small, weak team had won. It was only a practice game, it wouldn't enter the official record books, but they had earned their first victory. Suddenly he was ashamed for having doubted them, for having written off the game before they even got on the bus. There were some things that you couldn't predict.

He pushed his plate back, paid the bill, and shoved out

into the night air. The sky was full of stars.

He stepped into the elevator. His fingers hovered over the buttons. Christine was on the third floor. She wouldn't care about the game right now, not really. She would want to know how the babies were. He pushed "four."

When he arrived at the NICU, he went through the first set of doors and carefully disinfected his hands just as the nurses had instructed earlier. He yanked a blue gown out of the locker and pulled it on over his clothes. Then the paper hat, then the mask.

Different nurses were on shift now. They hadn't seen him falter, and it felt as if he was being given a second chance. One pink-capped woman nodded to him as he made his way to his children.

His daughter, barely more than a pound, wriggled in her glass case. He reached inside to stroke her foot. She startled, and he quickly drew his hand away. His son was still, possibly asleep, but his heart beat steady and strong. *Tsuyoshi.*

He touched the label on his son's incubator.

"Excuse me, nurse?"

The young woman tending the baby next to his looked up. "Yes?"

"Can I borrow a pen?" He took a deep breath. "I'm ready to give them names."

Polishing
the Halo

Polishing the Halo

Kelly Shimada sat amid a mound of pink-wrapped gifts, swaddled girl-baby sleeping on her lap.

According to Miss Manners, a baby shower was supposed to be held in the eighth month of pregnancy, but etiquette be damned; the members of the Foreign Wives' Club already put enough time and energy into keeping track of and adhering to Japanese customs (exactly how much to spend on a summer gift for one's boss, where to stand in an elevator, which days were inauspicious for hospital visits, and so on). Sometimes a little anarchy was just the right thing. Besides, Baby Shimada had been born fourteen weeks ahead of schedule, during the sixth month of pregnancy.

For days, weeks, months, she'd struggled in an incubator at the university hospital. But now she was home, healthy, and beautiful.

"She looks just like you," Trina Nishi cooed. "She's got

her mama's formidable eyebrows."

Kelly groaned. Better to say that her daughter had inherited her lotus-blossom complexion or gray eyes. But no matter. In truth, she loved hearing that the baby, Ana, resembled her. Her husband's relatives all claimed that she looked like their side of the family.

"Isn't it wonderful when she turns her head at the sound of your voice?" Elizabeth Tanigawa said.

Kelly forced a smile and nodded. She'd read in all the books how this would happen, but Ana was oblivious to her mother's coos and cajoling. She wondered if newborns were like ducklings, attaching themselves to the first face they saw, the first voice they heard outside the womb.

Ana had been rushed off to the incubator as soon as the umbilical cord was cut. Kelly hadn't seen her daughter until the next evening. For the rest of Ana's hospital stay, Kelly had spent hours of each day sitting beside her. She'd sung every lullaby and children's song that she knew, and talked to her about everything from her grandparents in South Carolina to the weather outside. Even so, the voices that Ana heard most often were those of the doctors and nurses who looked after her.

Lisa Miki, unofficial club leader, clapped her hands. "Let's get to the presents, ladies. And then we've got some games."

Kelly reluctantly handed the baby over to Trina to free her fingers. Once Ana had settled against her oldest expatriate friend, she picked up the first gift.

She stripped the pink-flowered paper away to reveal a CD from Elizabeth—classical music for babies.

"They say it'll turn your baby into a genius," Elizabeth said. She was known as the group "*kyoiku mama*," the education mother. Already her three-year-old son was enrolled in violin lessons, art classes, and swimming school. In another year she'd probably have him studying the abacus.

"Thanks." Kelly smiled at Elizabeth and began unwrapping the largest of the gifts—the gaudiest crib mobile she'd ever seen, a two-foot assemblage of fuchsia plastic flowers and cartoon characters.

"Don't you love it?" Trina gushed. Her passion for kitsch was renowned among the women. She always said that the thing she missed most about living in the States was going to garage sales. "Wind it up," she said. "It plays the theme to 'The Mickey Mouse Club.'"

Kelly'd had something more tasteful in mind, but the mobile made her laugh. It would be an ironic addition to the nursery.

The final gift, from Lisa, was a stuffed lamb with a big button where a navel might be. When the button was pressed, the lamb began emitting the sound of a human heartbeat.

"It'll remind her of the womb," Lisa explained. "It'll help her sleep."

"Thank you all so much," Kelly said. She felt tears well up; her hormones were still out of whack.

They were a small group, but they helped each other during good times and bad. These three women had supported her through the fear-fraught days of her daughter's beginnings.

Now, everything was all right again. Ana would become a genius via Mozart. She'd go to sleep to the soothing drum of a heart. Everything was fine.

A couple of weeks later, Kelly was in the shower, exulting in the flow of hot water over her tired-to-the-bone body. She pressed her nipples and marvelled once again at the spurt of milk. Then she moved her hand up further, to her armpit, and felt a lump.

A lump? It was probably a blocked milk duct or something caused by hormones. No doubt it would go away in a day or two.

But what if it wasn't? What if it didn't?

She felt her hair for shampoo residue and, finding none, wrenched the faucet. Water off, she shook herself free of drips and grabbed a towel.

The baby was sleeping. Her husband Takeshi was reading in bed.

She peeled away the towel and sat down beside him. "Feel this."

He looked up in surprise. "What?"

She grabbed his hand and pressed it under her arm. "Do you feel that?"

He worked his fingers around the tender skin there. "It's probably milk."

"But what if it isn't?"

He gently tugged his hand away and pulled her into his arms. "We've been so lucky, Kelly. Against all odds, Ana turned out to be a perfect little girl. Most babies born that early and that small don't survive. It's human nature to be suspicious of too much luck. It's normal for you to expect something bad to happen, but don't. Just be happy."

Kelly touched the lump again.

"If you're really worried, go see a doctor and get it checked out."

Two days later, the lump was gone.

Kelly played the classical CD for Ana and read to her as she lay in her crib. She tried everything from Sendak to

Shakespeare, Frank L. Baum to Baudelaire. She recited bits of *The Canterbury Tales* that were still stuck in her brain from high school and sang songs that her own mother had sung around the house—"How Much is that Doggie in the Window?" and "Downtown." Motherhood was, she realized, an epic journey into memory.

Kelly wanted to stimulate Ana as much as she could without exhausting her. She pressed Ana's fingers against different textures and took her for daily walks.

They lived near a tourist complex consisting of a *manju* factory, preserved farmhouses, a traditional garden, and an art gallery overlooking a pond of brightly colored carp.

On some days, Kelly pushed the stroller into the art gallery and tried to get Ana to look at the tapestries dyed with locally processed indigo or the woodblock prints. On other days, they took the tour of the *manju* factory, watching the freshly baked buns filled with sweet bean paste move along the conveyor belt, or lingered by the pond. When she and Ana appeared, the fish surged en masse to the surface of the water expecting feed. Kelly was a little frightened by their greedy, gaping mouths, but Ana waved her arms with excitement.

In the evenings, when Takeshi was home, there would be other sensations—scratchy whiskers, warm bath water, the scent of a father's neck.

Once Ana was asleep, almost nothing could wake her. She didn't even flinch when the first thunderstorm of the summer crashed in the night. She slept on, her tiny fists curled, her lips slightly parted.

Ana did not wake to thunder. She didn't even blink when they passed a barking dog on an afternoon stroll, though

Kelly nearly jumped out of her sandals. Six months had passed since Ana left the hospital, but she still did not turn at the sound of her mother's voice.

"I think there must be something wrong with her," Kelly told Takeshi as they sat on the sofa, watching their daughter.

Ana was on a blanket on the floor, batting at the toys dangling from her baby gym.

"She's just slow in developing," Takeshi said. "You worry too much."

He clapped.

Ana looked at his hands and smiled.

"See?"

At Ana's monthly check-up, Kelly expressed her fears to the pediatrician.

"We'll run a test," the doctor said.

Takeshi accompanied them to the hospital on the day of the exam. They had to wait on a padded bench in a long corridor until their name was called. Most of the other patients were elderly; they'd probably lost their hearing after a lifetime of music and laughter. Kelly looked down at the baby in her arms and felt a pang.

After twenty minutes, a nurse approached them.

"Mr. and Mrs. Shimada, right this way, please." She led them into a dimly lit soundproof room and gave Ana a sedative.

Kelly rocked her until she fell asleep, then laid her on a cushion on the floor.

She and Takeshi stood by, watching as the doctor, a young woman in a pink coat, attached electrodes to Ana's temples and forehead. The baby stirred when a big pair of headphones were clamped over her ears, then went back to sleep.

The doctor explained that the machine would monitor the response of Ana's brain to a series of high frequency blips. Then she set everything in motion, and left the room.

Kelly watched the lines squiggle across the monitor's screen. There was plenty of activity, she was sure. If Ana couldn't hear a thing, the lines would be flatter, wouldn't they?

When the test was finished, the doctor removed the electrodes and called them into her office. Kelly scooped Ana, who was just starting to wake, into her arms. She rocked her daughter as the doctor pointed to the squiggles on the printout with her ballpoint pen.

"I'm sorry, but there was virtually no response. From what we have here, I'd say that your daughter is profoundly deaf."

So this was it, Kelly thought. This was the calamity she'd been expecting. Of course it had all been too good to be true.

As they drove home from the hospital, Takeshi stared straight ahead, his mouth set in a grim line. "I never thought I'd be the father of a handicapped child," he said.

Kelly shivered a little. He hadn't said "Ana" or "my daughter" or "my princess." There was suddenly so much space between father and daughter, husband and wife.

The words "I'm sorry" flew out of her mouth. If she hadn't gone into premature labor, maybe Ana would have turned out all right. Somehow, her body seemed to be at fault.

Takeshi didn't answer.

Ana squealed in her car seat.

At the next gathering of the Foreign Wives' Club, Kelly waited for the right moment to break the news about Ana. She was aware that Takeshi hadn't told any of his friends about their daughter's deafness—maybe men didn't talk about things like that—but Kelly needed to share this information.

The four women met at a favourite coffee shop, the one that looked like a log cabin, kids in tow. Elizabeth's raven-haired son was quietly coloring a Pokemon character. Trina's kids were under the table, clawing at knees. Kelly held Ana on her lap.

Trina was wrapping up one of her hilarious tales about trying to find underwear in her size in Japan. Their laughter drowned out the Japanese pop music coming from the speakers. When things had settled down, Trina leaned over toward Ana and clucked her tongue.

"Aren't you the sweetest little baby?" she said in a high voice.

"She can't hear you," Kelly blurted out. "We had her tested. She's deaf."

The smiles died. Eyes dropped to laps.

Elizabeth was the first to recover. Oh, honey," she said, laying her hand on top of Kelly's. "Please. If there's anything we can do to help, let us know."

Kelly bit her lip, determined not to cry, and nodded.

"Things could have been so much worse," Lisa added. "She's perfectly healthy in every other way. She'll be fine."

"She can still be Miss America," Trina chimed in. "Or an actress like that woman who won an Academy Award."

"Sure," Elizabeth said. "She can do anything. I heard there's a deaf guy playing Major League baseball."

For a brief moment, Christine was comforted, but then she remembered that she had never in her life met a deaf adult. Trina and Elizabeth were referring to celebrities, but how did the average deaf person get by? How would she be able to protect her child if Ana couldn't hear her shouts of caution? How would she make friends? How would she find a man who could look beyond her disability and love her? And how would mother and daughter communicate? Christine would have to learn sign language, when she hadn't even fully mastered Japanese.

What's more, Miss America and the Major League baseball player weren't Japanese. Sure, there were opportunities for the disabled in the United States, where people were inclined to lobby and protest, but here in the land of *shikata ga nai*, where people were always shrugging and saying, "It can't be helped," what would someone like Ana be able to do?

Thoughts of the future were overwhelming and suddenly, even the sympathy of her friends was hard to bear. They didn't—couldn't—understand. Their children were strong and healthy. Hearing. Not only was Ana a girl in a society that favored boys, not only was she a mixed race child in a country that cherished pure blood, but also she was disabled.

She remembered reading about a famous Japanese writer whose son was severely autistic and how the neighbours had found their public appearances shameful. She also remembered visiting a school for special needs children along with the mothers of a group of normal preschoolers. She'd heard whispers of "How sad!" She wasn't looking forward to a lifetime of pity.

Were these women, her friends, thinking of how lucky they were? Was Elizabeth secretly grateful that she'd given birth to a precocious black-haired boy?

She excused herself from the gathering before anyone else and went home. Then she immediately went for the CD of classical music for babies and threw it away. She dug up a blues CD, one she hadn't listened to since her and Taekshi's trial separation in the early, tumultuous days of their marriage.

The singer's voice filled the house with melancholy, but Ana chirped happily in her high chair. She grabbed at rays of sun and smiled up into her mother's somber face.

For weeks, Kelly avoided her friends, preferring to weather her grief in solitude. She played with Ana, showed her pictures, gestured, and took her for long strolls as before. When elderly neighborhood women clucked their tongues at the baby, Kelly didn't bother to tell them that Ana couldn't hear.

And then one day, well into fall, when crisp maple leaves crunched underfoot, she pushed the stroller into the parking lot of the tourist complex.

A tour bus had just unloaded and men in navy jackets were busy snapping photos. A group of schoolchildren in uniform leaned over the carp pond, flinging bits of bread into the water. And then there was a family—a man, a woman, and a small girl in a gingham dress—preparing to get into a nearby car.

At the sight of a baby in a stroller, the mother and father paused and sauntered over. The father bent down and wiggled his fingers to Ana's delight. The mother smiled at Kelly. They didn't speak to her, but that was normal. Most strangers didn't expect her to be able to speak Japanese and so didn't even bother to attempt conversation.

Then the mother waved vigorously at the little girl leaning against the car and motioned her over. She pointed to the baby and moved her hand over Ana's head as if she were polishing a halo.

The little girl came running, the skirt of her dress belling in the breeze, and peered into the stroller. "*Akachan!*" she said. "A baby!"

The mother nodded and repeated the polishing gesture. Then she moved her fingers rapidly and the girl turned to Kelly.

"What's her name?" the girl asked in Japanese.

"Ana." Kelly realized then that the woman's gestures were words. She was communicating in sign language, and the little girl was translating for her. Her parents were deaf.

Kelly stood there while the three of them fussed over Ana and then watched as they got into their car. It was a perfectly normal car, and they were a perfectly normal family.

She waved as they pulled out of the parking lot and her eyes followed them down the road. More than anything, she wanted to race after them. She was eager to see their house, to see how they lived, to witness their everyday habits.

Instead, she held her palm over Ana's head and moved it around in a circle. She wondered at the meaning as she pushed the stroller toward home.

Bonding for Beginners

Bonding for Beginners

"Why does our daughter have to take a bath with her teacher?" Christine asked her husband. "As a Japanese teacher, please explain it to me."

They were driving along the mountains of western Shikoku, returning home after a weekend spent at a spa. They—Christine, her husband Hideki, and the twins, Emma and Yoshi—had indulged in a "family bath," a private hot tub under the stars. Bathing as a family seemed intimate and appropriate. After all of this time in Japan, she'd lost much of her American prurience. She no longer thought it was perverse for fathers to bathe with their young daughters as per Japanese custom. But Emma taking a bath with her teacher and unrelated kindergartner boys?

"Do you know Dewey?" Hideki asked. He stared ahead, his profile still almost as sharp as it had been at twenty-four, when she'd met him.

"As in John, the philosopher? Yes." Christine had once been a teacher, too. She'd probably studied the same pedagogical theories that he had, but learned to apply them in different ways.

"Dewey said that education should occur in all areas of life."

"Hmm. So you're saying it's an American idea."

She tried to wrap her mind around this, while thinking that the following weekend's school sleepover was a quintessentially Japanese activity. No one in her native country would think it necessary for a four-year-old to bond with her classmates, at least not to the degree that was intended. Emma would be cooking, eating, sleeping, bathing, and doing just about everything else with her group, the Stag Beetles.

The weekend was intended to be a family event, but Christine was supposed to stay out of the way. She and her son would be eating at another table, sleeping in another room, bathing at another time. It seemed odd and unnatural to Christine to let the teacher help Emily brush her teeth and shampoo her hair instead of having her mother do it.

When she'd first told Hideki about the sleepover, he'd said, "You should cancel." He wouldn't be going himself because he had a game. He was a high school baseball coach, in addition to being a P.E. teacher, which meant, in Japan, at least, that he had virtually no time off. He certainly had no time for deaf school events or concerts and festivals at their son's preschool.

But it quickly became clear that everything at Emma's school, the Tokushima School for the Deaf, was geared toward the sleepover. Three weeks before, the first orientation meeting was held. The three, four and five-year-olds in the school's kindergarten, were divided into groups the children named themselves—the Ghosts, the Melons, the Stag Beetles. From that moment, they ate lunch in their groups every day. Almost every school activity—making curry and rice, cutting bamboo branches for the festival of Tanabata, decorating the branches with paper cut-outs—was conducted as a group.

The mothers were suddenly spending all day together, too. It was Deaf School policy that the mothers of the three-to-five-year-olds hang around until their kids were ready to go home. "In case something happens," Nishioka-sensei, the head teacher, had explained. Most of the mothers whiled away the hours in the designated Mothers' Room where there was a coffee maker and a microwave and a long low table surrounded by cushions.

Christine wasn't used to kneeling for hours at a time, and besides, she didn't want to sit around chatting when she could be doing something more useful. What did she have in common with the other mothers anyway, besides a deaf child? Their children didn't have cerebral palsy, like Emma did. They didn't have to think about wheelchair access every time they left the house. And they didn't experience every day as an exercise in cross-cultural communication—at least, not with each other.

Most of them were at least a decade younger than Christine. They'd all been born and raised in Tokushima. Only a couple of them had ever been abroad—one to Guam, on her honeymoon, another to Hawaii with her family the year before. Another woman's husband traveled frequently for business—to Egypt, Saudi Arabia, and India—but she had never left the country herself.

Several of them had gotten married because "they'd had to," or maybe they'd just hurried the inevitable along. In the

Mothers' Room, the youngest ones bragged about their youth. Once a week there was some conversation about sex (birth control, or maybe frequency thereof) and another about dieting, although they were mostly as slender as bamboo.

Christine had lived in Europe for awhile before she came to Japan. She'd traveled in Third World countries. Before that, she'd lived in four different states. She'd had a lot of boyfriends in her twenties, a few tumultuous relationships she thought she'd never get over, but when she met Hideki, something had gone still at the center of her. She'd first been taken in by his untameable curls, his kind eyes, the lines that rayed out from them from so much smiling. Later, she'd been moved by his sense of social justice. Before he became a base-ball coach, he'd volunteered with underprivileged kids in the next town over, the ones whose ancestors were butchers and tanners and undertakers, descendants of untouchables who still felt the sting of prejudice.

Christine's decision, after four years of knowing him, to marry and settle in Japan, had been careful and deliberate. They hadn't wanted kids right away, or at least she hadn't; Hideki had gently proposed starting a family as they downed a bottle of Dom Perignon on their first anniversary, but she'd wanted to travel a bit more and write a novel. When the twins had finally been born, they had been planned and wanted.

Christine had come to Japan originally to teach English. Her students had been eager to wring every possible bit of native speaker syntax and American culture out of her. They asked her opinions about Japan-U.S. trade friction, the bases in Okinawa, 9/11, and they wrote down what she said. The mothers at the deaf school, however, did not seem at all interested in Christine's point of view, and she avoided referring to her previous life in Michigan or France because she didn't want to appear pretentious.

She realized that she could have tried harder to fit in, but that she didn't really want to. When there weren't any meetings about the sports festival or the bazaar or the sleepover or whatever, Christine would sometimes slip away and go for a walk in the park at the center of the city, or even duck into a café and read a magazine. She always felt a little guilty when she returned. The mothers would look up in something like surprise when she pulled the sliding door open. Sometimes she wondered if they talked about her when she wasn't there.

The day after the family trip to the spa, after spending half an hour wandering among the blooming roses in a corner of the park, she felt a little guiltier than usual. She opened the door to find all of the other mothers cutting out colorful felt shapes and threading needles. She nodded a greeting, and made an effort to wedge herself into the circle. They were making name tags for the sleepover.

"What should I do?" Christine asked, trying to appear eager. If she were Japanese, she would know. She would just plunge in.

Akaishi-san, mother of Miki, a girl in Emma's class, handed her a few scraps of felt. "Stitch these brown pieces onto the yellow one."

Christine craned her neck to see what the others were doing. One had almost finished sewing a brown felt stag beetle onto a small square of yellow.

"Oh, this stitch is too big," she said. She began to tear it out.

Christine wanted to roll her eyes. Who cared if one teeny tiny stitch was not exactly the same as the others? Wouldn't this time be better spent studying sign language or lobbying for an elevator? (There were several students, including Emma, who couldn't walk, but the three-story school didn't have any ramps or elevators.) She could already tell that this was going to be a week-long project. They would spend more time making the name tags than the children would wearing them. But that was the wrong attitude. She should admire them for their attention to detail, for their insistence on perfection. They were doing this for their beloved children, after all.

Sewing was a way to demonstrate their affection. Isn't that what the head teacher had preached at the beginning of the school year when she'd ordered the mothers to make the required tote bags and aprons for their children by hand?

"What's the stitch?" Christine asked.

"Chain."

How did that one go? Back in the day, when she'd been a Girl Scout, she must have learned all those stitches—the slip stitch, the satin stitch, the chain stitch. But her hobbies ran more to reading and travelling and studying foreign languages than embroidery. Now, she was stumped.

"So does everyone here know how to do the chain stitch?" Christine asked.

The women looked at her—six pairs of dark eyes filled with scorn (or so she imagined). She could almost see the speech bubbles over their heads: "A woman who doesn't know how to sew. Hmmph. Well, what do you expect? She's American."

"We learned it at school," Miki's mother finally said.

"Oh, really?" Christine had to have someone teach her. She tried, she really did, but her stitches weren't even. Everyone would know which one she'd made.

Later in the day, after they'd all had lunch followed by green tea, the head teacher, Nishioka-sensei, appeared with a stack of print-outs about the sleepover. As usual, she handed out copies to everyone, then proceeded to read every single word aloud, something that never ceased to annoy Christine. With the exception of herself, they were all literate, and responsible enough to read the pages on their own.

One of the sheets featured a chart showing the names of the participants and every father's estimated time of arrival. Some would be dropping by after work, others were coming after the bonfire on the beach, in time for a parent and teacher drinking party. Next to Hideki's name (actually, "Emma's Father"; they only existed in relation to their children, apparently), there was an X.

Another paper listed participants' duties. Every task had been designated, down to who would put the smallest children's hearing aids in airtight cases at bedtime and who would wield the hair dryer after the bath. Christine had volunteered to spread a blue plastic sheet on the ground before dinner, thinking it was something she wouldn't mess up. How hard could it be? They were all going to eat outside, under the tall pines in front of the Youth Hostel, within earshot of the whispering sea.

The next page was of the bath schedule. Emma, Christine noted, would be going in just after dinner. Everyone was allowed twenty minutes in the bath, from start to finish. There was a photo-copied image of the bath as well—a large room with a tiled floor and a tub the size of a small pool. They would sit on small wooden stools to wash with soap outside the tub, then rinse and soak in the nearly scalding water.

A final sheet listed exactly what items the children should bring and exactly how they should be packed—each outfit in a separate see-through plastic bag, each bag labeled: pajamas, change of clothes, after the bath. They were to bring a small pack of tissues, a handkerchief, a plastic bag for the shells and stones that they would collect at the beach on the last day. The plastic bag was supposed to go in a pants pocket.

On the one hand, Christine was impressed by this attention to detail. On the other, she hated it. Living in Japan brought out her inner adolescent. She often felt that the teachers were trying to control her daughter's entire life and she wanted to rebel.

Even before Emma was born, she'd had a pretty good idea of how involved teachers were in their students' business. After all, she'd taught English as an extracurricular subject in public schools and she knew about the yearly visits teachers made to students' homes (and just how nervous this made the mothers, who spent days cleaning and fussing over what sort of snacks to serve). Plus, her husband was a teacher. More than once he'd been called away near midnight to deal with a student caught drinking in a karaoke box, or shoplifting at a Lawson's convenience store. If one of his forty home room students was in the hospital, he was obliged to visit.

She'd thought the teachers' involvement excessive and ridiculous then, but now that she was on the other end of it, she found it unbearably intrusive. The Deaf School produced reams of memos telling parents what time to put their children to bed, what they should eat and drink, what kind of books they should read, on and on, as if they parents themselves had no common sense. Meanwhile, among themselves, the mothers were hypercritical of everything the teachers did: This one only used finger spelling as opposed to proper sign language. That one had no idea of how to discipline unruly four-year-old deaf boys.

When Christine brought Emma to the school for early intervention, back when she was three, she packed a lunch— sometimes sandwiches on whole wheat bread with a side of potato chips, which she quickly learned were beyond the pale. *Snack food.*

"What does she drink with her lunch?" the teacher asked one day, eyeing Emma's imported Bob the Builder thermos.

The teachers ate in their own room. Christine, Emma, Miki, and Miki's mother, ate in the classroom together.

"Water," Christine answered, pouring out a cup.

"Mineral water?"

"No, just tap water."

The teacher frowned. "You really shouldn't give her tap water. She could get food poisoning."

Was this woman for real? Christine glanced at Miki's mother, expecting a look of mutual disbelief but Akaishi-san quickly looked away. What was the big deal? She knew that the local water was potable; she'd been drinking it for ten years. It's not like the Ganges was gushing through their pipes. She was too taken aback to argue, though, so she said nothing. Red-faced, she listened as the teacher complimented Akaishi-san for giving her daughter cold barley tea: "I hear it's really healthy."

After the teacher had gone off to her own lunch, Miki's mother leaned forward and said, "You don't give her carbonated drinks, do you?"

Remembering all this made Christine want to rant about the caffeine in the tea the older kids were given at lunch. Instead, she sipped her own green tea till she felt calm again.

They finished making the name tags with a few days to spare, but then the mothers had to rehearse a dance. On the evening of the sleepover, everyone would perform by the light of the bonfire. The children were practicing skits. The mothers, it had been decided, would sing and sign a Hawaiian song. The mother of Rai, a five-year-old boy who'd recently gotten a cochlear implant, was choreographing the whole thing. Miki's mother had designed costumes—hula skirts with strips of colored plastic hanging from the waistband.

It was July, hot as dragon's breath, and humid, too. The deaf school, like every other school in Tokushima, had no air-conditioning. In the Mothers' Room there was an oscillating fan, but it gave only the suggestion of relief. It was in this room, in this heat, that they pulled the plastic skirts over their clothes and practiced moving in unison, hips swaying as their fingers formed words.

Christine could feel rivers of sweat soaking her T-shirt. After they'd run through the song a couple of times, there was a discussion about the final moves. Should they drop to their knees and throw their hands in the air—"ta da"? Twirl? Bow? None of this mattered to Christine. All she wanted to do was throw herself into the cool pond across from the rose garden.

That Saturday, Christine packed the car with bags, thermoses, and twins. Then, with gritted teeth, she set out for the sleepover. Although she jammed a reggae tape into the cassette deck, the only song in her head all the way there was "Kamehameha," the one that she'd heard over and over in the Mothers' Room for the past few days.

The Tokushima International Youth Hostel was at Omiko Beach, a popular spot for barbecues and ocean swimming. "Don't think hotel," the head teacher had warned. Christine told her son it would be like camping. When she entered the building and made her way up the dark stairs, she had a flashback to all the five-dollar-a-night European hostels she'd slept in on her junior year abroad. The stained pillows and futons make her cringe now. These days she was more of a Nikko Hotel kind of person.

Christine and Ken found that they'd be sharing a room with Miki's mother, her five-year-old sister and baby brother. The room was empty except for a small coin-operated television on a table. The bedding was stashed in the closet. It smelled vaguely of mold and cigarettes.

Emma, of course, would be sleeping down the hall on futons with the other Stag Beetles, and her teacher. For a moment, Christine imagined teacher and children curled up together like kittens and felt a stab of jealousy. She'd never spent a night so far apart from her daughter.

After stashing their bags and thermoses, they returned downstairs for a meeting. Emma was already with her group. Christine tried to catch her eye, but her teacher seemed to be blocking her from sight on purpose. Well, she was supposed to be paying attention. This was an extension of school, after all. Christine sat down at the back and pulled Yoshi onto her lap.

Next, everyone moved to the picnic area to begin preparing curry for supper. There was an open pavilion under the pines with grills and workspace.

Emily's job was to peel the onions. Christine could see her sitting in her purple wheelchair, pulling the papery skin away. She was intent on her task, oblivious to her mother's watchful eyes.

Now that dinner was underway, it was time for Christine to spread the blue plastic sheet on the ground. She found it in the meeting room and, after clearing away a few sticks and rocks, laid it out on the pine-needled ground. Here and there were little hills of plastic, and Christine stamped around in her stocking feet, tamping them down. It was a small job, but she couldn't help feeling that she had done something wrong. The Japanese mothers would lay it out perfectly and they would know if she had not.

Finally, she shook her head in disgust. She was becoming paranoid. The blue plastic sheet really did not matter so much. She looked up, then, for her son. He was nowhere in sight.

Maybe he'd wandered down to the beach, she thought. He was normally very outgoing, quick to organize games at the park with kids he'd never met, the class "mood-maker" at his own preschool, according to his teacher. Christine wandered through the pines, calling out his name. She scanned the groups making curry—the Melons, the Ghosts, the Stag Beetles—looking for Yoshi's chestnut head. Then she looked again toward the water and her heart began to bang.

"Yoshi? Where are you?"

"I think I saw him go into the hostel," Rai's mother called out.

Christine ran toward the building. She found him alone in their room, drinking from his thermos in the fading light of late afternoon, and nearly fainted with relief.

"What's wrong, sweetie? What are you doing in here?"

He dropped his head to his chest. "I feel shy," he said.

He doesn't feel like he fits in, Christine thought. *Like me.* She ruffled his hair and pulled him close. "Well just sit here for a little while," she said.

Later, as they sat on the blue plastic sheet with their bowls of curry, Christine looked across at her daughter, eating with her teacher. She was smiling, shoveling in the food like it was the best thing she'd ever tasted. The other Stag Beetles signed something to her that Christine didn't understand, and Emma nodded and signed back.

She's having a great time, Christine thought. She wondered if her daughter understood that she would be reunited with her family when the weekend was over.

Christine watched as Emma, assisted by her teacher, washed her bowl and spoon. Then the teacher pushed Emma in her wheelchair to the hostel for a bath. Christine imagined the teacher's fingers tangling in her daughter's long hair, squeezing out the shampoo suds. She had a vision of the teacher's hands sliding over Emma's soft skin, into her crevices and hollows, the tender way she might blot the girl's back with a towel. She remembered how, just after Emma and Yoshi's premature birth, she had stood by as the nurse swabbed their bodies clean in the incubators. She hadn't been allowed to hold them without permission. It had taken such a long time to feel like their mother.

After dinner, when they were all once again assembled in the meeting room, Nishioka-sensei announced the beginning of the *Obake Taikai.*

Yoshi looked up at Christine with alarm. "Ghosts?"

"Just people dressed up as ghosts, sweetie. The mommies and daddies will be wearing costumes. They'll be giving out presents."

Yoshi shook his head vigorously, tears already pooling in his enormous brown eyes. "I don't like ghosts!"

"Okay, we won't join in." Christine's heart sank. She at least wanted to see Emma's thrilled expression. Her daughter was the brave one, her son the hyper-imaginative cautious child. Sometimes, like when Hideki dangled Emma upside-down over a pond, she wondered if those shrieks of delight

weren't abnormal. Maybe her lack of fear was another mani-
festation of brain damage. Being afraid of the ghosts in the
woods at dusk (or talk of earthquakes, or being swung by the
ankles) seemed normal for a kid of that age.

They watched the other kids and mothers and teachers
embark on the ghost hunt, and then Yoshi turned to go back
to their room. Christine sighed, wishing she'd brought a
picture book or pack of cards to amuse him with.

The final event of the evening, before the children were
sent to bed, was the bonfire on the beach. If this were
America, Christine thought, they'd sit in a circle around a
teepee of kindling, prepared for marshmallow roasting and
singing. But this was Japan, and the campfire was referred to
in the printed schedule as a "firestorm." She anticipated something grand and theatrical. Yoshi was biting his fingernails.

Plastic sheets were laid over the sand. They would sit
there, away from the fire, and watch. When everyone had
gathered, Rai, master of ceremonies, stood up at the front of
the group and announced the start of the fire ceremony."

Some fathers laid fat logs in a square.

"Look!" One of the teachers directed everyone's attention
further up the beach. "The goddess of fire is coming."

Nishioka-sensei, wearing a mask and headdress, was
advancing with a torch and two attendants, also in costume.
It reminded Christine of the Olympic ceremony, or some
ancient Mayan rite. The teacher was well disguised and she
wondered if the children actually believed that she was really
a deity.

The "fire goddess" lit the logs, slipped away into the
night, and the main attraction began. Each group—Ghost,
Melon, Stag Beetle—had prepared a skit. Christine knew that

the kids had spent weeks practicing, just as the mothers had. The air was filled with nervous tension.

Emma and her group took their places on the sand. They were wearing costumes made of strips of plastic. Emma held a tube of tightly rolled paper that was probably meant to be a wand or a sword. Other than that, Christine had no idea what was going on. In the dark, with the chirr of crickets and cicadas filling the night, it was difficult to make out the children's imperfect pronunciation and to follow their sloppy signs. But no matter. Emma was smiling, pleased as ever, to be onstage and the center of attention.

For the finale, Christine and the other mothers shimmied into their hula skirts and lined up in front of the fire. With the Hawaiian music blasting from a cassette player, they swished and swayed together under the sequinned sky. It was fun, after all; Christine found that she couldn't stop smiling.

She'd meant to join the other parents for drinks in the meeting room after she got Yoshi to sleep, but she'd nodded off herself. When she did wake, in the early hours of morning, Yoshi was hogging her pillow and crowding her off the futon. For such a fearful boy, he slept in an attitude of absolute trust—arms flung open, belly exposed.

On the other side of her, Miki's baby brother had rolled off his own mother's futon and nestled against her back. Christine carefully nudged the children, clearing some space for herself, and tried to go back to sleep.

In the morning, Christine and Yoshi dressed and packed up their belongings then headed downstairs for breakfast. Emma was already in the dining room with her teacher, spooning up scrambled eggs. Christine noted, somewhat ruefully, that her daughter's pigtails were tighter and neater than usual, her part perfectly straight. She herself felt rumpled after a night spent fending off thrashing toddlers. Yoshi was sleepy and sullen.

After breakfast, the plan was to go down by the water and explore. Nishioka-sensei had scissored her fingers in the sign for crab and shown the kids pictures of water insects they might come across. There might be shells, too, she said, and interesting rocks.

They all set out in a loose column along a well-trodden path. But instead of continuing to follow the path, which was bordered by railing, Nishioka-sensei veered off through the underbrush, down a steep slope to jagged rocks below. There were no steps, but a few fathers were positioned to give a hand to anyone who might need help getting down.

Christine was surprised to see that Emma, who could not walk, who would never be able to make it safely down such a treacherous incline by herself, was already on the rocks, grabbing at frogs and beetles. She realized that the treads on her sneakers were worn flat and that she would probably slip. Yoshi, at her side, had grown stiff with fright.

"We'll just stay up at the top of the hill and watch," she murmured. "Unless you want one of these nice daddies to help us get down there."

He shook his head, already working his way back to the official trail.

Before she went after him, she took another look at her daughter—happy, curious, poking between the rocks, leaning down for a closer look at a bug.

Emma could do worse, Christine thought, than to spend her life among these people. She watched as her little girl caught a crab with her small fingers and held it up to the sun.

Between

Between

It started with corn. One of their new neighbors, a bent-backed woman with a face like that of those apple dolls Lisette had made long ago when she was a Brownie in Michigan, had rolled into the driveway on a bicycle with a paper bag full of fresh-picked corn. Corn brought back more memories of Michigan, of sitting on the back porch with the bushel baskets before her, husking and detasseling with her mother, of suppers at the picnic table under a parasol on the patio, of sweet yellow kernels shiny with butter, studded with salt crystals, summer in her mouth.

Lisette bowed awkwardly to the neighbor, whose name she hadn't quite mastered, mumbled a thanks in Japanese, and then brought the cobs into the house. She stood at the sink peeling back the green leaves, stripping the silky strands, while Kai played with blocks in the next room. He was talking to himself while he played, narrating in Japanese. Sometimes

he played in English. It seemed to depend on the context—
for instance, English when he was pretending to be
Spiderman, Japanese, when he was imitating a ninja.

When she'd cleaned the corn, Lisette gently tugged a
cookbook off the shelf. It was tattered by now, the middle
pages now loose sheaves; she had consulted it over and over,
looking up recipes for meatloaf, macaroni and cheese and
chocolate cake, in order to comfort herself when she felt
homesick. Now, she flipped to vegetables, then to corn: Add
one tablespoon sugar and one tablespoon lemon juice to each
gallon of water. Heat to boiling; boil uncovered 2 minutes.
Remove from heat; let stand 10 minutes before serving.

She followed the instructions, and then she prepared a
salad with cucumbers and tomatoes that another neighbor
had brought over the day before, and grilled a fish. When
supper was laid out, she called Kai to the table. Isamu
wouldn't be home till later; he usually ate alone.

Lisette admired the colors—the yellow of the corn, the
cucumbers with pine-green skin, the flash of red tomato. Her
mouth watered. Kai slid into his chair.

"*Itadakimasu*," they said, their palms pressed together.

She tried to put a cob of corn on Kai's plate, but he held
out his hand as if he were stopping traffic. "I don't like corn."

"You should try it with butter and salt," she said. "It's
really good."

It was then that he shook his head and said, "Japanese
don't eat corn like that."

Lisette sighed. The summer fifteen years ago when she'd
first arrived in Japan as an assistant English teacher, she'd
been instructed on many occasions about the peculiarities of
the natives. Her boss, a middle-aged woman who'd just
returned from a four-day trip to visit Beatrix Potter's birth-

place, had laughed when Lisette complained about the incessant shrill of cicadas.

"We Japanese find the sound beautiful," she said. "Japanese hear insect sounds in a different part of the brain than foreigners, you know."

She'd wanted to challenge the woman. Which foreigners? Does that include the Chinese? Koreans? Japanese-Americans? But being new to the country, she'd kept her mouth shut and nodded politely as if in agreement.

Another time, on the way to watch a *bunraku* puppet show, they'd passed a Western hamburger restaurant and the teacher had frowned saying, "We Japanese have shorter intestines than you foreigners. We can't digest meat as easily as you."

It was as if she believed her countrymen were of another species entirely.

Lisette had felt both annoyed and excluded whenever the teacher made these kind of pronouncements. Now, in the dinette with her son, she said, a little bit more coldly than she intended, "Kai, there are many ways to eat corn." She picked up a cob and took a big bite.

Or maybe it had happened later, during their trip to South Carolina to visit Lisette's brother and his family. She remembered, though, what Kai had said in the car, on the way to Osaka to renew his American passport that fall.

Isamu had been driving. Lisette laid back against the headrest, looking out the window at the tiny islands scattered across the Inland Sea. She listened to father and son talk, glad to not be, for once, the center of Kai's attention.

"So which do you like best," Isamu asked. "Soccer or baseball?"

Lisette smiled. She knew what their boy would reply. They both knew. He was, even at five, a diplomat, and his dad was a baseball coach.

"Baseball!"

"Who do you like better? Mommy or Daddy?"

Kai giggled. "I like Mommy *and* Daddy."

"Are you American or Japanese?"

Kai paused for a moment, then said, "When I'm in Japan, I'm Japanese. When I'm in America, I'm American."

Good enough, Lisette thought. When he was twenty, he would have to choose sides, unless the law changed. But for now, he was a dual citizen.

They were a bit confused by all of the one-way streets in the city of Osaka, but they finally found the consulate, just down the road from a Portuguese restaurant. When they'd gone through the glass doors and up the elevator, Lisette leaned down and whispered in Kai's ear, "You're in America now."

The navy passport that arrived in the mail a week later was the same size and color as his Japanese passport. But this one listed his middle name—Benjamin, after his grandfather, Lisette's dad—and gave him rights to a country that his father didn't have.

Two months later, Lisette and Kai set out for the United States. Isamu stayed behind, and Kai cried for a few minutes about leaving him at the gate.

"Pretty soon you'll be able to play with Max," Lisette said, hoping to distract him.

Max was her brother's son. He was a year older than Kai and they'd gotten along well on previous visits.

And this visit started out well enough. Max was there to greet them, as soon as they walked in the door. "I'm going to be a rocket scientist or the president when I grow up," he said. "What about you, Kai?"

Anne, Max's mother, leaned in and said, "Excuse him. It's Career Week at school, and he's all fired up. By the way, I volunteered you to speak to Max's class about being a writer. The day after tomorrow. That's okay, isn't it?"

"Uh, yeah. I guess." Lisette didn't really think that the kids would want to hear about the kind of writing she did—rewriting manuals for electronic goods in the middle of the night when her family was fast asleep. Once, long ago, she'd published a few poems in her college's literary journal and she'd even started a novel or two, but she could hardly call herself a writer. Then again, maybe she could just talk about Japan. Surely kids would be interested in hearing about life in a foreign country. She could talk about volcanoes and sumo wrestling and how the Japanese kids ate whale meat in their school lunches. They'd get a kick out of that.

In spite of the fourteen-hour time difference, Kai recovered from jet lag in only a couple of days. It must be because of all that fresh air and wide open space, Lisette thought, watching her son through the window. He and his cousin were running around the expansive back yard, dodging between fat, towering pines, and rolling around on the plush grass. Oh, what Lisette wouldn't give for a lawn like that.

At home in Japan, they had just enough room behind their house for a sandbox and a patch of grass. They had a skinny maple and a quince tree that bore heavy, hard yellow fruit Lisette couldn't figure out how to eat.

That evening, Lisette's brother Pete fired up the grill out

on the big wooden deck overlooking the lawn. Lisette remembered how their father had grilled steaks on the back patio every Sunday. How she had missed that smell.

In Japan, they owned a small hibachi, but Isamu said that the smoke from a barbecue would disturb the neighbors, so they rarely used it. They only grilled at the beach, or at the riverside where dozens of other families did the same.

Lisette watched her brother tend the hot dogs until they were plump and oozing juice. Then she helped Kai fix a sandwich.

"Look at that," Pete said, as Kai bit into the bun. A bit of ketchup was smeared on his face. "He looks just like an American."

"He *is* an American," Lisette said. "He has an American passport."

"Well, why don't you get that husband of yours to move over here? There's a Japanese auto plant in the next town over. He could get a job there easily."

Kai put down his hot dog then and scowled.

"He's a teacher," Lisette said. "And he loves what he does."

"He could teach, then. He could even coach Little League."

Lisette sighed. Her family believed that anyone would be happy to live in the United States of America, land of plenty, land of opportunity. And it was true, she missed her home country and her family. But she wasn't sure that Isamu could ever be truly content outside of Japan. Sure, he loved the cheap golf, but here, he stumbled through conversations and didn't get jokes. He was more confident in his own country.

Lisette glanced over at Kai, who was still frowning at his plate. She gave him a small smile.

"Our home is in Japan," she said.

Kai picked up his hot dog and started eating again.

At Max's school, Anne, Lisette and Kai went into the office to get visitors' passes. Lisette was pleased to see big, leafy plants and an aquarium full of fish. And the colors! The walls, the furniture, even the teachers' clothes were in shades of yellow, orange and red. Such a bright, cheerful place!

Anne led them down the corridor to Max's classroom where the eighteen kids sat at two long tables. Lisette was pleased to see that they came in all shades. There were at least two children of African descent, another couple who appeared to be Mexican-American, and an Asian girl, maybe Vietnamese.

Mrs. Brown, the teacher, who had emigrated from Mexico herself, greeted them at the door. "Everyone, let's welcome today's special guests," she said. "Max's aunt and cousin have come all the way from Japan."

"They don't look Japanese," a blond boy said.

Mrs. Brown let the comment pass, but Lisette felt Kai stiffen at her side.

The children gathered on a bright green carpet and Lisette settled in a chair. Kai knelt beside her. She'd brought along a map and a picture book about a Japanese boy. She held up the map and indicated a few key spots—Tokyo, Mt. Fuji, and Nagano, site of the winter Olympics. Then she Kai point out the island where they lived. After she read the book, she asked the children if they had any questions. A few hands shot up.

"Did you write that book?" the Asian girl asked.

"No, I'm sorry. I didn't."

"Have you ever seen a volcano?" another kid asked.

"No."

"Do you have a kimono?"

"Uh, no."

They seemed increasingly disappointed. Max, there in the back row, looked embarrassed. She felt like a failure.

Finally, Mrs. Brown stepped in. "Let's all give our special guests a big hand!"

Lisette stood and bowed and they were escorted from the room.

Later that evening, Anne put a hand on Lisette's arm and led her into the next room.

"Why don't you rest? I'll call you when dinner's ready."

Dozing on the sofa, she could hear bits of Max and Kai's play. At first, they were pretending to be firemen, but then Max said, "Hey, I've got an idea. I'm George Washington and you're a British soldier."

"George Washington?" Kai asked.

"Don't you know? He was the first president."

Lisette's stomach went a little queasy. Was he supposed to know about the Founding Fathers? The Revolutionary War? Had she known that in kindergarten? Then again, Max was fairly precocious. She knew that he was beyond picture books, and that he entertained himself by writing poems and stories on the computer.

Lisette felt a twinge of jealousy. She'd done everything she could to interest Kai in learning to read English. She'd even set up a chart for him: a star for every ten minutes spent practicing writing the alphabet, a small toy for every ten stars, and an expensive computer toy—the one that his best friend had with the fighting beetles—if he mastered the stack of easy readers she'd bought for him. Bugs and violence—she was willing to stoop that low just to get him sparked. But it hadn't worked. He'd learned to read Japanese with almost no help at all, and now he sat in rooms with books by himself, sounding out the words with greater and greater proficiency.

She'd done her best to fill him in on American culture, though she had felt he was too young to learn about war. He sometimes asked her about photos on the front page of the newspaper, and she answered evasively. He was never allowed to watch television news. But now, she could hear the "bang bang bang" in the next room as "George" took out the soldier.

Lisette was leafing through an American parenting magazine ("How to Fire Your Nanny," "Time Outs for New Moms") when Kai suddenly appeared, brow furrowed, chin against his chest. His lower lip jutted in a classic pout.

"What's wrong?" Lisette put down the magazine, which didn't tell her how to raise a bicultural child in Japan, anyway, and patted the cushion beside her.

Kai burrowed into her side. "I want to go home."

She sighed. Home was living so close to others that you could hear the phone ring three doors down. Home was having her mother-in-law telling her how to store her broom and chiding her about the dust on top of the television. Home was not understanding half the things that people said. Here, Kai was, in a huge house full of playthings, with a yard big enough for a full-scale soccer game, a treehouse, cousins who understood his love for Scooby Doo and macaroni and cheese. Why wasn't he having fun? Sure, he missed his father, but it had to be more than that.

He plucked at the cushion for a moment then looked up at her. Tears pooled in his eyes. (His father's eyes, she had to admit.)

"Max said that there was a war between Japan and America."

"Yes, there was, but it was a long time ago. Japan and

America are friends now. Daddy and Mommy got married, right?"

He sniffled and dragged a sleeve across his nose. "Max said that America won and Japan lost."

Oh. So that was it.

"Well, honey, I don't think anyone really wins a war."

She could have told him how Japan had been rebuilt, how it was now a prospering and peaceful country, but all that she could think about was his apparent rejection of his second country, her country. Even as he sat there snugly, warmly against her, his hand toying with hers, she felt disowned.

Kindergarten had already started up again when they got back to Japan. Kai would be going into a new classroom, with a new teacher, and kids he didn't know who'd had a jump-start on bonding. She hoped that the foil-wrapped chocolate rabbits Kai was bringing as souvenirs would help him break into the group.

She parked the car and walked him to the gate. Some mothers lingered there, chatting after their kids had gone inside.

"Hi, Lisette!"

She turned to see Phoebe, another American mom with a Japanese husband. Their daughter Erika was in the four-year-old class.

As they stood there catching up, Lisette caught sight of a little girl with frizzy blonde hair. Her name hadn't been stitched onto her uniform yet.

"Hey, who's that?"

"Her name's Zelda. Her father is a visiting professor this semester. He's teaching American literature."

Lisette watched the girl for a moment. She stood still, at the center of a swirl of children, looking as if she might cry.

"Sato-sensei put her in with Erika," Phoebe said. "I guess she was hoping Erika would be her buddy, but you know how they are about speaking English in front of their Japanese friends."

Lisette nodded. A lump formed in her throat. She'd heard of bicultural kids asking their foreign mothers not to go to their Japanese schools. It was embarrassing for them to stand out, embarrassing to hear the calls of *"gaijin da!"*

The rest of the day, Lisette worried about Kai. She imagined him sitting alone on the playground, or lost in confusion as the teacher reviewed the ideograms she'd taught during Kai's absence. But that was silly. They wouldn't be studying Japanese characters till first grade.

She drove to school to pick him up a little earlier than usual. A few mothers were already waiting in the shade of the gingko trees.

At the sound of the bell, the children started filtering out the door. Erika rushed out, into her mother's arms, and then Kai, like a greyhound out of the gate.

"How was school?" She bent down to look into his face, checking for trauma. "Did they like the chocolate bunnies?"

"Yes! Everybody said 'thank you.'" His eyes darted around as he waved to his new friends. "Bye Ichiro! Bye Ami-chan! Bye-bye Zelda!"

"You met Zelda?"

"Yeah. She's from Michigan, like you, Mommy. She likes roast beef and her favorite animal is the kangaroo."

"You talked to her?"

"Yeah. We played together, me and Zelda and Junpei. She

doesn't know any Japanese words, so I had to tell everyone what she was saying."

Lisette felt a burst of pride. "You were a translator."

"Yeah." Then suddenly he spun away from her.

She watched him go, out into the world.

www.ingramcontent.com/pod-product-compliance
Lightning Source LLC
Chambersburg PA
CBHW031418250626
47155CB00004B/1535